The Baker and the Bookmaker

MOST IMPRUDENT MATCHES
BOOK TWO

ALLY HUDSON

Busy Nothings
Books

Digital ISBN: 979-8-9882181-2-8

Print ISBN: 979-8-9882181-4-2

Library of Congress Control Number: 2023916959

Cover design by Holly Perret, The Swoonies Romance Art

Copy and Line Editing by Rebecca Sanchez, Once Upon an Editor

First edition

To Bryton.
Thank you for the dedication you show toward the care and feeding of your introvert.

If you're afraid of butter, use cream.

— JULIA CHILD

The Baker and the Bookmaker

Prologue

CANDLELIT APARTMENT OVER HUDSON'S
BAKERY - JANUARY, 14 1816

"THE FIRST TIME I saw your mama, I thought of the sunset. Her burnt orange, fire red, and honeyed gold curls swirled together in a riot. She had them trapped in a mauve silk ribbon, but they fought their way free. The last stand of the sun before the night takes it over."

"I didn't know I married a poet," my wife whispered from the nearby bed.

"Only when I think of you," I replied, before turning back toward the sleeping bundle in my arms. My daughter frowned, her face scrunching in displeasure. Before she could let out a wail, I leaned back, setting the rocking chair back into motion under the moonlit window. She settled, and I continued. "I thought she was pretty then. I didn't have the words, not at four years old. Even now, I don't possess the vocabulary to express the dazzling loveliness of her."

"Oh Augie, do be serious."

"I am perfectly serious, my sweet sunset. Now, where was I?"

"Apparently, writing sonnets about a flour-covered four-year-old to our daughter."

1

"Yes, of course. I met your mama on one of the saddest days of my life. Since then, she's supported me on all my worst days. Better still, she's been the one responsible for all my best days. Today is the most wonderful of all. It brought me you."

"You're going to tell her this entire story?"

"Of course."

"Not all of it, I hope," she murmured tiredly.

"Every bit of it."

"Not the engagement eve, that's inappropriate. Or that day at the club," she chided.

"I'm just setting the expectation for her future husband."

"The expectation is that he takes more than twenty years to—"

I cut her off before she could remind me of my very occasional foibles and the one or two opportunities that I missed. "Hush you. Shouldn't you be resting?"

"Yes, but my husband has lost his mind," she said with an eye roll before settling farther back into the pillows.

I rocked my daughter quietly, waiting for my wife to drift off so I could continue my story.

With an irritated huff, my wife opened one eye. She made a *go on* gesture with her hand, before curling up on her side.

My smile was clear and bright in my voice. It was impossible to be otherwise with this little girl in my arms. "Less than a week before I met your mama, something terrible happened..."

One

"Now, Augie, you're to stay in the big house today, remember? You'll mind Mrs. Hudson?" Papa asked as though he hadn't reminded me three times last night.

I nodded solemnly in response. Everything I did was solemn that week. My nose was reddened, cracking, and sore from the handkerchief. Food held little appeal, and my stomach ached with a horrible combination of hunger and unbearable sorrow. Mama was gone.

A few days ago, Papa set me down between my sobs and explained the plan. While he worked, I would stay in the kitchens of the big house where the cook, Mrs. Hudson, could mind me along with her own daughter, also four years old.

He clasped my hand in his hot, rough one, so different from the delicate warmth of Mama's, and guided me down the familiar path toward the big house. As stable master for the Grayson family, Papa had been given the little cottage close to the horses. I was familiar with the outside of the big house. The inside was a mystery soon to be solved. We passed by the lake and the big oak tree, but instead of taking the usual turn into town, we rounded the back of the house.

Papa knocked brusquely on the solid door. It opened to reveal a stout, ruddy-cheeked woman with red hair and a bright smile. She ushered us in through the scullery to the main kitchens.

To *her*.

Her back was to me, that little girl with the sunset hair. She stood on a heavy wooden chair struggling to reach the worktop, even with the chair's assistance. A dusting of flour fell over her and the surrounding area like snow.

Elbow-deep in some kind of dough, she slipped as she tried to push the rolling pin before steadying herself.

I didn't know it right then, but in that kitchen, covered in flour with her fingers in dough, was her favorite place in the world.

Vaguely, I heard Papa introduce me to the cook. But the girl had turned toward me. What could be more important than that?

She hopped off her chair, sending a cloud of flour through the air. After wiping her hands on the edge of her apron, she offered me a graceless curtsy. My heart jolted at the sight.

Papa coughed, pointedly reminding me of my manners. I gave her my most dignified bow. I hadn't mastered the motion, and it was certainly stilted. She flushed the prettiest shade of rose pink. It shone through the layers of flour and freckles dusting her nose and cheeks.

Off to the side, I caught the sound of laughter from the adults. It was irrelevant. I had just discovered the girl's eyes. They were a greenish-gray color with flecks of brown in the very center. *That* was essential information.

A curl managed to free itself from the ribbon, and she tucked it behind her ear. And I fell in love.

"Augie, this is my daughter, Anna," Mrs. Hudson explained from somewhere in my periphery.

Anna. A name perfect in its simplicity. Her heart-shaped

face and sweet smile didn't need the embellishment of some showy name.

Papa's heavy grip landed on my shoulder, turning me toward him, ripping my gaze from her. "Heed Mrs. Hudson. I'll be back to collect you at supper."

I nodded, solemn once again. He led me to the nearby table and pushed me down on the bench seat. Then he slipped back out the way we'd entered.

Spinning back to Anna, I found her already returned to her chair and dough. The sunlight streamed through the window in front of her. The light caught her copper-red strands and a strawberry-gold halo appeared around her head.

She rolled the dough with her entire body, nearly slipping from the chair once or twice more in her efforts. Each time, I lurched from the table as though to catch her, but she righted herself before my services were needed.

At length, her mother came and took the trays she'd prepared, moving them to the ovens. Anna dusted herself off, brushing the flour from the worktop into a pile before sliding it into a waiting dust pan.

Once again, she hopped off her chair, then danced over to the bench across the table from mine. She settled there, prim and silent, watching me with interest.

I then realized my fatal mistake. Seized with indecision, I floundered for words. How could I decide the first words I would offer the love of my life? It was a great deal of pressure at four years old.

Interrupting my panic, Mrs. Hudson set a plate of Shrewsbury cakes on the table between Anna and me. The scents of spice and sugar wafted from the plate. For the first time in five days, my mouth watered. I was hungry. Not just hungry—ravenous. With little more than a distracted "Thank you" to Mrs. Hudson, I plucked a cake off the tray. I popped the entire thing into my mouth and chewed once, twice, before swallowing it nearly whole. Then I grabbed a second. A third. After the fifth, I lost count.

Anna rescued one from my feast. She took bite after delicate bite.

"Do you like them?" she asked. Her voice was light and lilting, like that of a songbird.

Between greedy bites, I mumbled an affirmation. Later, I would realize my error. Her first words from me were rumbled out between full cheeks. Hardly the romantic image I intended to project.

"I made them," she added.

I froze mid bite. The delectable, delicate morsel in my mouth had been crafted by her hands. I looked down at the plate, now nearly empty. After swallowing the contents of my overfull mouth, I took another bite. This one was slow, intentional. I considered the spices, the hint of something floral, the buttery softness and airy texture.

"They're the best thing I've ever tasted," I answered.

That earned me a pleased smile and a peal of laughter. Even her laugh was lovely, light and free.

The rest of the day was spent in pursuit of that sound. I was desperate to hear it again, longer, louder, fuller.

When my father returned to collect me that evening, I realized tears had abandoned me today. Gone from the moment I experienced my sunset for the first time.

Two

THORNTON HALL, KENT - NOVEMBER 28, 1790

THWACK... thwack... thwack... Storms of dust exploded on impact and swirled around the carpet beater with every whack.

A pair of tiny booted feet swished back and forth from the same oak branch my rug was hung on. Seeking a laugh out of the owner of the feet, I reared back and smacked the carpet again with all my strength, purposefully following through and spinning in a rapid circle.

The sweetest giggle rang out from the tree. "I think that one's done. Is that the last of them?" Anna called from her perch atop the branch.

"For today. She's got us doing every rug in the house twice a week."

I scrambled up the trunk, stepping on the knots we had already worked out. Understanding my plan, Anna slid farther down the branch and came to a stop atop the rug.

As I plopped down just slightly too close to her, she released another peal of laughter at the sight of me. Gently, she ran her fingers through my chestnut hair, swishing them around. Her actions kicked up another cloud of dust and threw my heart into a flutter.

In retaliation, I brushed an imaginary dusting of flour off her cheek, tutting performatively. I wanted to loosen her braid and mimic her motions, but I knew it would be too far.

Autumn was in the air, and the tree's leaves had begun to adopt Anna's colors. Reds, yellows, and oranges fell from it in every gust of wind, swirling around her in a poor imitation of her curls.

She slipped farther away at the sound of approaching footsteps. Glancing around the trunk, I saw Michael trudging along.

The viscount's ward, Michael Wayland, had been given a place of honor in the household. He was treated like a son. As he rightly should have been. Because there was really no question that he was the viscount's illegitimate son. He was the spitting image of his father. Dark, wavy hair topped equally dark eyes and a crooked smile, just like the viscount.

Anna and I saw little of him, though we were the same age. Or so it had been until *her*.

A few weeks ago, the viscount had married. The new Lady Grayson was a tall, pleasant-enough looking lady. But her gowns were showy with too many baubles and too much frill. She smelled of decaying lilacs, and her mouth was permanently pinched, as though she had smelled something foul. George, one of the footmen, jested that no one had told her the smell was her.

And she loathed Michael. In less than a day, he had gone from favored ward to something beneath her shoe to be squashed.

I would never forget the day I made my way into the kitchens from our cottage and found him sitting half-slumped over the table with his head in his hand.

His eyes were red-rimmed, and an uneaten bowl of porridge cooled in front of him. There was no doubt as to the cause of his displacement. Agatha.

In mere days, the woman had gone from being respectfully referred to as Lady Grayson by the staff to a hissed Agatha with a tone of exasperated disdain. Such were her demands on the staff and her general attitude toward everyone.

Behind the boy, I could see Anna, flour-coated and nodding her head at him as though I was supposed to fix this. How she expected me to do that was unclear. After all, it wasn't as though I could turn back the clocks and have his father marry someone less horrid.

With a shrug at my Anna, I went over to the counter where today's delight was cooling. Tarts, lemon. Perfect. Those were the ones he stole when he snuck away to the kitchens between lessons.

Scorching my fingers, I snuck a few onto a plate before spotting the raspberry ones. My favorites. I grabbed a few of those, too, sacrificing more of my skin. After dropping down beside him, I set the plate on the table between us.

"I'm Augie, Augustus. My pa is the stable master."

"Michael." His throat was hoarse, and he wiped his nose with his sleeve. He made no explanation for his presence. It was unnecessary.

"Want one of Anna's tarts? They're the best!"

"Anna?"

Hearing her name, she turned from her dough and offered a flour-coated wave and a small smile.

"You bake the tarts?" he asked. At her nod, he continued, "They're very good. I especially love the lemon ones."

"I know. Those are the ones you steal," she retorted with a grin. He ducked his head.

"I steal the raspberry ones," I added, plucking one off the plate and taking a bite. The crust was tender, flakey, and buttery, and the bite of the raspberries offset the sweetness perfectly. My camaraderie seemed to perk him up slightly, and he grabbed a lemon tart, accompanying me in a bite.

He joined us every day after. Once his lessons were finished, he would find his way to the kitchens, assisting where Mrs. Hudson would allow and providing companionship where she wouldn't.

"Michael!" Anna called when he spun aimlessly, searching for any sign of us. He saw us and scurried his way up the tree, using the same knots I had. Finally, he settled on the branch across from us.

"What did you learn today?" Anna asked. Michael had shown us some of his lesson books a few days ago and started to explain some of the things he'd been taught.

"Some arithmetic. And a bit of reading."

"Which do you prefer?" I asked.

"Both," he answered distractedly. He was fixated on something near the top of the tree. "Everything is better than history. Do you ever climb higher than this? I bet you can see Margate from up top."

"We're not allowed higher," Anna explained.

"No one will care if I go," he said. After standing up on his branch, he gripped another branch higher up. Pressing his knee to one just below that, he pulled himself up.

"They most certainly will care if you break your neck!"

"No, they won't. Agatha will throw a party." Another branch, higher and higher he went. There was honestly no retort for his comment. Agatha probably would celebrate his demise.

Higher still he climbed, ignoring Anna's worried protestations. Finally, he was nearing the top when he settled on a branch and threw his leg over it.

"You two should come up! You can see the whole estate."

I was about to agree to follow him up before Anna answered for us both. "Absolutely not!"

"Did you know there's a creek? And, oh! Raspberry bushes. Just on the other side."

"You cannot possibly tell if those are raspberries from that height."

Just after another of Anna's protests, we heard the ominous aching crack of wood giving way. My heart jolted. We waited, silent, for the inevitable crash.

When none was forthcoming, Michael reached to grab a nearby knot. That tiny motion was enough. The branch he was sitting on broke with an angry snap.

Dangling from his hold on the single branch, he gave a wordless cry. I couldn't recall the journey to his side, only that one second, I was beside Anna watching in horror, and the next, I was trying to pull him to the branch I had found just below him.

It took a bit of maneuvering, but I managed to gather him by the waist and get his legs over the same, more solid, branch. Finally secure, he was pale and shaking slightly, his hands shredded to ribbons and a laceration across one eyelid. But he was otherwise unharmed.

"You saved me?" he questioned in a quaking voice. I wasn't certain why it was a question.

"I did?" I asked back, hoping for clarification.

"Would you two get back down here?" Anna asked. She stood beside the trunk on the ground. I gestured for Michael to go first, and he reluctantly swung down to the next branch.

His descent was much slower and more carefully considered, but eventually he made it to solid ground, and I followed.

Anna inspected each of us thoroughly upon our arrival at her side and fussed over Michael's hands and rapidly swelling eye. "If you think I'm going to make tarts out of the raspberries you found over there, you're sorely mistaken. I don't make tarts for boys who purposefully endanger themselves."

"But, Anna..." I mumbled.

"But, Anna, what? And no lemon either."

"But..." Michael added.

"I won't tell Mother. But I'm not going to reward you with tarts either."

Michael and I shared a look. I had written sonnets to Anna's tarts. Going without them would be a hardship—Michael apparently agreed with me—but facing Mrs. Hudson's wrath...

"How long?" I asked.

"A month," she replied primly.

"Deal," Michael said. He helped me pull the rug off the branch and held the end while I began to roll it up.

"No deal! This is me doing you a favor."

"And we thank you very much," he answered.

"You two are going to get into so much trouble. Aren't you?"

"Almost certainly." Michael laughed as we trailed after Anna.

Three

AFTER THAT DAY, we were inseparable. Eventually, I learned to speak coherently in Anna's presence with minimal gawking —most of the time. And Michael became more servant than ward with every passing day.

Mornings were spent watching and occasionally assisting in Anna's art. Flour, sugar, water, and yeast combined in hundreds of new ways to make incredible confections. By the age of six, we all knew the truth. Anna was destined to own her own bakery. Her pastries would be the talk of the town.

And we weren't the only ones who thought so. Michael had convinced his tutor to give lessons in the kitchens. Anna and I joined whenever we were able, learning arithmetic and reading, anything she might need for her bakery. Everyone knew great things were in her future, and she would need those skills along the way.

Our evenings became more interesting as well. The older footmen had taken to teaching us games of chance. I was certain their intention had been to hand over some of their unwanted tasks to us. Unfortunately for them, Michael took to each game with more alacrity than the last. He lost so rarely that one or two of the men were convinced he was a cheat and refused to play against him. Until a few shillings were tossed onto the table. Money had a way of making sensible men senseless.

Such was the case this evening. Michael won round after round of hazard, even in his distraction. And he was distracted; we all were. Maids ran to and fro with buckets of water and fresh linens. Or worse, soiled linens. George, a footman a few years older than us, nearly fainted at the sight.

Every few minutes, an agonized shriek escaped from upstairs. They were coming more regularly, with less time between each. And we all knew what they meant.

Michael tossed the dice with a gritted jaw when another scream escaped, nicking.

"So, what happens to you when she pops out a boy?" George needled before taking a hearty swig from his flask.

"What do you mean?" Michael asked, his tone stark with irritation and raw nerve.

"Well, if she has a boy, there's no need for you. Is there?"

"There's no need for me now. I can't inherit."

"Well, it's just... He could legitimize you. Couldn't he?"

"That's not how it works. That babe in Agatha's belly, if it's a boy, is a future viscount. If it's not... I'm still just a ward. The title would go to Father's cousin."

Rolling again, he nicked once more, to the consternation of George. He was probably asking the impertinent questions to upset Michael and throw him off.

It wasn't working. Nothing did.

"That must smart," George added.

"Leave him alone. No sourdough for you if you're going to be horrid," Anna replied. She was glorious as always. And her sourdough was exceptional. The homey scent of it in the oven wafted through the kitchen.

"Why would it smart? You're not going to be a viscount, either. Does that bother you?" Michael asked.

"You're a lot closer to viscount than I am. And you're about to be replaced by an infant. You think Agatha will allow you to distract from the heir?"

"George," I warned through gritted teeth.

Michael won again, while another wail pierced the kitchens. This one was followed by a quieter, angrier cry. A babe.

The butler, Weston, scurried into the kitchen a few minutes later. "A boy," he proclaimed with pride. "Master Hugh Henry Grayson," he added, then scurried back out the way he'd come, as though his news was merely exciting and not life-changing.

Every eye in the kitchen was on Michael. "Five," he said and rolled once again. And it was five.

They watched him a moment longer before returning to their previous occupations. All except Anna and me. We heard the hollow note in his voice. She nodded at him, expecting me to do... something.

I didn't know how, precisely, she expected me to fix this. It was as he said; Michael hadn't actually lost anything. At least nothing tangible. He wasn't any less a future viscount now than he had been this morning. But there was no doubt how this story ended. Not with Agatha for a stepmother. Not now that there was an heir. Michael would be lucky to have a bedroom come morning.

One by one, everyone abandoned the kitchens until only the three of us remained, Anna appeared by Michael's side, a plate of sourdough with butter in hand.

"A crust of bread, Anna. Really?"

"Well, it'll be all you have to live on when she throws you out. Best get used to it," she retorted with a teasing smile. "I even brought you butter."

"Very generous." In spite of the sharp retort, neither of us was willing to forgo Anna's bread.

Michael buttered his while I ate mine unadorned. The sour taste with the bubbly texture was magnificent. Sourdough had taken Anna a few attempts to perfect—according to her anyway. I thought the first loaf was delectable, even if the crumb was uneven. Now though, it was incredible.

We ate in companionable silence, long after we should have been asleep. It wasn't entirely uncommon for me to sleep in the servants' quarters, so Papa would be unconcerned.

"I want to go see him," Michael announced, breaking the silence.

"You want to see him?" Anna asked, the desperate hope that she had misunderstood him clear in her eyes.

"He's my brother. I should get to see him. Shouldn't I?"

Anna looked at me, wide-eyed, worrying the corner of her lip between her teeth. Her two front teeth had fallen out, so she was utilizing the ones just to the side. I adored the rare appearance of her gap-toothed grin. She had taken to smiling with her mouth closed once she lost the teeth, so it was a treat. She nodded at Michael again, breaking me from my reverie.

He wasn't strictly wrong... But Agatha wouldn't see it that way. Still, he should meet his brother, and if Agatha was asleep, all the better. "Let's go."

Anna gave me an exasperated eye roll before putting up the bread.

Together, we crept up the back stairs to the third-floor nursery. The door was cracked open just enough to peer inside. There, in the center of the room, bathed in moonlight from the window, was little Hugh Grayson, future viscount.

Anna caught my hand and reached for Michael's, but she was too late. He pressed the door open and slipped inside. Swaddled in a blanket, the baby cooed softly at the disturbance.

"Michael!" Anna hissed into the darkness. Her little hand was more than enough to keep me planted by her side.

Michael approached the crib, peering over the side. "Hello, Hugh. I'm Michael. I'm your brother." From afar, I saw a tiny hand peek out from the blankets, reaching up to grab Michael's outstretched finger through the bar. "I'll teach you everything. How to ride and fence. How to play hazard. It will be fun. And I'll keep you safe. I promise."

My heart gave a pathetic jolt. His words were far from what I expected. Until that moment, I hadn't realized the full extent of what Agatha had taken from him.

A sharp, cold hand clasped my shoulder, yanking me around. The night nurse. "What are you two doing here? And you! Get away from the baby!"

Michael, having startled at the commotion, smacked an arm against the crib while pulling away. Hugh let out an irate cry.

"Waking the baby. Just wait till I tell the mistress about this." She shoved past me into the nursery and grabbed a squalling Hugh. "Go on, git! You'll be lucky if you don't get a lashing in the morning," she called after us. "Come here, sweet boy. Don't cry. It's all right." That last bit was directed at the crying babe as we stumbled down the stairs together.

Back in the dim light of the kitchens, Michael finally broke. The tears were gentle, quiet, and when Anna wrapped her skinny arms around him, entirely muffled.

In the morning, we received the most thorough tongue lashing I would ever receive. Agatha ordered an actual lashing as well, but no one was willing to dole out the punishment. Instead, we were ordered to look pained and pathetic when she was near. It seemed to suffice.

As the days grew longer, Hugh grew larger, and the incident was forgotten by all but the three of us. That night transformed our friendship from childish camaraderie to a bond that could withstand distance, time, hardship, and anything else life had to offer.

Four

THORNTON HALL, KENT - DECEMBER 11, 1801

WITHOUT REALLY NOTICING, Anna and I fell into the roles of housemaid and footman, respectively. It was generally assumed I would become a footman, groundskeeper, or the like. Anna, though... she should have been working in a bakery, gaining more experience so she could open her own someday. Instead, she was doing the work of both a kitchen and scullery maid—and sometimes a downstairs maid if Agatha had scared off the latest hire.

There was less time for baking and for watching her bake.

Today, though, I was watching her sugar cakes in the oven for her. It had been weeks since I'd seen the dusting of flour on her nose. And it was far too long since one of her confections melted in my mouth.

She had just finished putting them on trays when one of the maids required assistance upstairs. The yuletide season was in full swing, and we had all been charged with various decorating duties.

Even with more limited time, Anna's creations had only improved. She had plans to decorate these cakes with icing in

19

festive patterns. It was one of the reasons she was allowed to forgo some of her usual duties in the name of holiday spirit.

My mouth was already watering. She had sprinkled sugar on them before settling them in the oven, and it had caramelized just a bit. The sensual note mixed with the dash of cinnamon she'd added. The scent was designed to torment me.

Over the last few minutes, I'd begun to have fantasies. If I said a single cake had fallen off the tray, Anna would have no way of knowing it had fallen off the tray and into my mouth. The dream of frosting was the only thing that kept me from forsaking my assigned duty.

Out the side window, I could see and hear the sounds of fencing practice. The viscount's two young sons, Hugh and the younger, Tom, were facing off against each other. It wasn't a particularly interesting fight since Tom was but five, and Hugh was nine. Little Tom barely reached Hugh's shoulder.

Michael had managed to swindle his way into attending the lessons and occasionally receiving his own. The fencing master was awful at cribbage.

His lack of participation didn't ease the tittering admiration from the maids. Apparently, he was quite handsome in his fencing costume. I didn't see it. He was the same scrawny Michael in the lamé that he was out of it. Honestly, he was only a few inches taller than Hugh, hardly a majestic sight.

It didn't matter though. They all thought him the most handsome of gentlemen, even the maids several years his senior. I rather suspected the attraction had to do with the rumors of the fortune he would inherit when he reached his majority—hogwash, of course, all of it. I once heard he was set to inherit a Scottish castle and a barony. I didn't know much about the title and property inheritance practices of the gentry, but even I knew that was ridiculous. Aside from already possessing the requisite heir and spare to inherit, the estate was in trouble.

Anyone paying the slightest bit of attention could see that the viscount could hardly pay his existing bills. An inheritance for his ward was out of the question. Each week our pay came later and later. Servants who left hadn't been replaced, and the rest of us just made do. Mrs. Hudson, and occasionally Anna, had to adapt recipes for fewer ingredients. Repairs were needed in the stable for going on two years now that hadn't been touched.

None of it stopped the maids from gathering in the scullery and peering out the door, naming their future Wayland children.

One of the cakes was near the edge of the tray. Without permission, my thumb reached out to brush against it. If it perhaps slid off the tray... Well, certainly that would be justification. I intended to wait until she'd decorated them. Really, I did. But they were so tempting. And I did like it when she scolded me.

The maids giggled at something I couldn't quite catch. One of them, likely Mary, called out, "Anna! Isn't he the most handsome of gentlemen?"

I didn't know it in that second, but that question would haunt me for years.

"Isn't who the most handsome of gentlemen?"

"Michael, of course!"

"Well, yes. I suppose he is quite handsome. But shouldn't you three get to lighting the fires?"

Three little letters were all it took to crush me. Y-e-s.

Of course, it was Michael. He was handsome. At least, if one liked a broody, well-educated sort of fellow. Even without a substantial inheritance, he was sure to have enough to help her open her bakery.

It would be a good match, a brilliant one in fact. If the mere thought caused my stomach to twist and my heart to give an angry thump, well, that was my concern.

Obviously, he would marry her. It was unfathomable that anyone in the world wouldn't wed Anna given but half an opportunity.

The fact that I had not considered this fate, that I hadn't thought... It was almost laughable. The three of us, growing up the way we had, and with a girl like Anna... It was inevitable. She was smart and kind and funny—only a dolt wouldn't have foreseen it. And that dolt was me.

She swept into the kitchens, smelling of pastry and pine needles as she brushed past me to the trays of cakes. She moved with the same graceful ease she always had, as though nothing had changed, as if all my dreams weren't in tatters in the scullery with the giggling maids.

I had no defense but to avert my gaze, checking the batch in the oven even though I knew they weren't finished. With the pointless task completed, I inspected the ones I'd removed earlier at her instruction.

"You didn't sneak any? Are you feeling quite alright, Augie?"

I swallowed back my despair. "Quite." It was more of a croak than a word, and she turned toward me with concern. I had to clear my throat in a false explanation. "I was waiting for frosting."

I forced a smile onto my face. It felt false and misshapen. But her mother returned from the market, arms laden with purchases, and we broke away to set the kitchen to rights. My heart would not be so easily righted.

Five

LESS THAN A WEEK after my greatest nightmare was realized, one of the maids decided to make it all so much worse.

She had placed mistletoe in every corner of the downstairs. Michael had already been caught underneath more than once. That was actually quite amusing.

He blushed all the way to his ears when Mary—the culprit herself, I suspected—trapped him there. She yanked him down to her and gave him a good one, tongue and all. He hadn't known what to do with his hands, so they'd kind of flailed about in the air around her before he used them to pry her off. She told everyone who would listen that he pulled her aside and professed his love afterward. He told me her tongue was a bit like a slug in his mouth. Accounts varied...

Some of the older footmen were angling to get her back under and give her a real kiss. George, in particular, was very explicit about what he would do to her. Most of it involved pressing his lips between her ample bosom and blowing to see if they jiggled. Even my most obscene thoughts of Anna, and they had become quite obscene in recent months, hadn't involved making her breasts jiggle. Touching them? Yes. Tasting them? Certainly. Any number of other things the older servants talked about behind closed doors that sounded less... silly? Absolutely. I was fairly certain, in spite of being two years my elder, that George was a little bacon-brained.

In the eleven years I'd known Anna, she had only grown more beautiful. Her hair was longer, silkier, and it had developed deep crimson undertones like twilight. Instead of dampening the sunset, it was more vibrant for the variation.

Her eyes were deeper too, a mossy gray-green perfectly offset by porcelain cheeks and just-bitten lips. Even though I knew she had feelings for Michael, visions of catching her under the mistletoe refused to leave me.

Somehow, I had convinced myself, despite all logic to the contrary, that a kiss would change her mind. If I could kiss her, even once, she would feel all the things I felt. My affection for her would transfer through our lips. I had never kissed a girl before, but I knew it deep in my bones—one press of our lips together and Anna would be as in love with me as I was with her. And Michael would be forgotten.

Of course, fate had other ideas.

Michael, desperate to escape Mary's continued attentions and those of at least three others, rose from the long, scarred wooden table to retire early.

There, right in the doorway to the kitchens, he bumped into Anna.

Underneath the mistletoe.

My heart tripped, devastated as I watched the end of my hopes. Michael had nearly knocked her over. He had to catch her around the waist to keep her upright. Anna flushed nearly as red as her hair while her eyes searched the room, presumably seeking privacy for this, their first kiss.

Her wide, green eyes met mine and her flush deepened. Certainly, she did not wish to cause a rift in our friendship.

Though it cost me everything, I gave her a small smile—the best I could manage.

She should be happy. He would treat her well. He would give her all the things I never could. I wouldn't stand in the way of her happiness, not for anything.

Her gaze flitted away, cheeks still flushed. Michael, ever the perfect gentleman, gave her a delicate kiss on the cheek. He probably wanted to save their first kiss for a more private venue.

I felt sick in a way I hadn't since Mama passed. I needed air, quickly, before I embarrassed myself more in this kitchen.

I stumbled, pushing past a few people, and made my way to the external door. A milk crate sat just outside. We often used it for a chair. I leaned against the house before sliding onto the crate, boneless and weary. My elbows fell to my knees, and my head dropped between them.

The December night air was sharp. I could nearly taste the snow that was sure to fall by morning. I was making a valiant effort to regain control of my breathing when the door beside me opened. Laughter and warmth from the ovens rushed out with my new companion.

George—not who I would have chosen to witness my humiliation and subsequent fall to pieces. He leaned against the building beside me. "So, Anna?"

I merely groaned pathetically in response, not certain I could open my mouth without emptying my stomach.

"I understand, but she's not for you. She's something special. She's got big dreams, and she's meant for something better than this. You'd do better if you set your eyes on someone like Mary or Julia. Someone like you. Someone who belongs here."

I shut my eyes against the certain truth of his words. Hadn't I always known? My sunset Anna. Could a man ever possess the radiance of the sky? Touch the sun? And if he could, should he? Would it not dim the sky's brilliance? A cloudy day.

"Here, this will help dull the sting a bit, I expect."

He handed me a flask. Until that moment, I hadn't had a sip of drink except at mass. I took a deep swallow and nearly spit it back out, choking.

"Yeah, it's whatever is left in the glasses after they finish upstairs."

"That's disgusting."

"But effective."

I could only hope he was right as I took another swig, more careful this time. It burned less the second time around when I knew what to expect.

The rest of the evening only came back to me in pieces. Huge swaths would never return.

I remembered the press of lips on mine. Mary's, I thought. Possibly her hand grasping my bottom. I recalled losing the contents of my stomach in the rose bushes. I remembered waking up, face down, on the large wooden table. Michael was at my side, whispering so loudly he needn't have made the effort.

"I didn't know what else to do with him," someone, perhaps George, muttered.

"Not letting him continue to drink didn't occur to you?" That was Michael's familiar drawl.

"I didn't think it would affect him that much. Or that his swallows were so large."

"I'll take care of him. Get to bed. And no more of your concoction. Unfinished drinks are to be disposed of."

A grumble preceded the click of the door. I tried to sit up, but the room started spinning the opposite direction when I lifted my head. I dropped my head back down; I preferred it clockwise.

"Augie? Are you going to be sick?"

"No." I couldn't keep the bitterness from my tone, and I didn't care to, not now.

"What happened?"

"Nothing. Everything. I don't know, but my life is over."

"That's unfortunate."

"She's never going to want me. I'm not good enough for her."

"That seems unlikely. Who are we speaking of?"

"No, you don't understand, Michael. She's the sunset, her hair—it's so pretty, just like the best sunsets. And she always smells so good. So good. Like pastry." I was fairly certain I stumbled over the word "sunset," adding another *s* or two. The point remained, though, so I wasn't concerned.

"Who has pretty hair and smells of pastry?"

"Anna." I drew out her name, feeling the syllables form in my mouth. It required concentration due to my numb tongue and lips, but her name deserved all my efforts.

"Ah, I should have known."

"Yes, you should have. You're going to marry her. The least you can do is 'preciate her pretty hair, gold and orange and red —like the sunset."

"So, you've said. But why am I marrying Anna?" he asked, like it wasn't obvious.

"Because she loves you, of course. And she smells like pastry."

"Anna loves me? That seems unlikely, but I'll play along."

"She does. I heard her say it. She said you were 'quite handsome.'"

"Finding me quite handsome hardly equates to marriage. Can you drink this?"

He handed me a full glass of water, and I tried to sip without choking.

"Yes, but of course you want to marry her," I explained.

"Because of the pretty hair and pastry scent. I've heard something to that effect."

"And because she's so talented. She's so talented, Michael. Have you tasted the things she bakes? They're so good."

"I have actually, and you're quite right."

"And she's kind and smart and funny."

"You've sold me on the match. I'll propose tomorrow," he decreed. "After I get you to bed... Can you keep quiet? Or are you still enumerating Anna's many fine qualities?"

"Still enumer-merating."

"Excellent! We'll wait until you're finished."

"You have to promise to treat her right. And make sure she gets her bakery. She should have her own bakery. She shouldn't be a housemaid, especially not here under *Agatha*."

"I promise, should Anna and I desire to wed, I will treat her like a duchess. Can we try to get upstairs without waking the entire household?" He helped me stand and dragged my arm over his shoulder. It was a scrawny shoulder. I don't know what Anna saw in it.

"All right, but I won't forget that you promised."

"I wouldn't expect anything less," he answered. "We're at the stairs now, can you step up?"

I made a gallant effort and reached the landing before I had to rest. Michael left me to lean against the wall.

"You're going to feel this tomorrow," he said. "I'll give your excuses, but I expect you'll still get a talking to from my future mother-in-law."

"Who?"

"Mrs. Hudson, Anna's mother. Remember? You decreed that we wed."

"Oh yes. She'll be such a good mother-in-law too. You're lucky."

He raised an eyebrow at that before he agreed with a shrug. Michael pulled me off my wall and braced me once more against his shoulder. With a sigh, he dragged us both up the final staircase.

"I'll ask her to go easy on you, but I suspect it will be in vain," he said. When we finally made it to my room, he all but poured me into my bed. "I'm not undressing you. Are you feeling sick at all?"

I shook my head for far longer than necessary, watching the room sway until it caught up with my eyes.

"All right, I'll see you in the afternoon. I expect you in your Sunday best for my nuptials. We'll hold them until the evening just for you."

Flopping down, I pressed my face into the pillow. "I hate you." He seemed to interpret the mumbled statement through the fabric well enough. At least, if the answering chuckle was anything to go by.

Death was an apt description for my constitution the next morning. When I finally made my way to the kitchens, I was met with a plate of Christmas fruit cake and a large glass of water. My name was on a slip of paper beside it in Anna's flowery handwriting. Few of the staff could read, but the sentiment must have been clear. I munched slowly, feeling the headache dissipate with each bite.

When I finally recovered enough to look around the kitchen, I saw that every bough of mistletoe was gone. The efforts were enough to repair the smallest crack in my heart.

Six

THORNTON HALL, KENT - JANUARY 24, 1803

WHY COULDN'T I wake up? This was certainly a horrid dream that would end as soon as I woke. Some part of me knew, though. I knew this was real. From the moment Michael glanced out the kitchen window toward the lake and saw the body in the water, my life would never be the same.

Mere seconds that felt like endless days between the moment he glanced up from the plate of lemon tarts we were fighting over and when I dragged him from the bank.

His wordless cry startled both of us. He was out the door before I noticed his movement. My gaze tracked his race outside, and I knew. Anna's startled shout barely registered behind me as I chased Michael down to the pond.

I slipped on the wet morning grass more than once. By the time I made it to the water's edge, Michael was tugging the body toward the bank. I grabbed him by the forearm, hauling him up out of the muck and dragging him onto the frost-covered grass. Anna was already unfurling blankets—I could only assume she'd had the presence of mind to grab them on her way out. She made a desperate attempt to warm Michael, rubbing his shoulders through the blanket, using a corner to dry his head.

I looked toward the body still in the muck. The viscount.

I knew my efforts would be in vain, but I flipped him over. Gone. The near-freezing water had been efficient.

Michael's stricken "Augie" was enough to shake me to my core. He knew without words there was no hope, no chance.

Anna choked back a distressed sob, redoubling her attempts to dry Michael and trying to coax him into the warmth of the kitchens. There was no hope for the viscount, but Michael had to be near frostbite, at best. I rose to assist her, to guide him back inside when I inadvertently nudged the body. Then the situation became so much worse.

A large rock fell from the viscount's sodden pocket. When I moved my foot away, another escaped its confines. I stared, uncomprehendingly for what seemed an eternity, my sluggish mind desperately seeking an alternative explanation for the facts in front of me. None was forthcoming. I reached back down, checking the additional pockets. Each was heavily weighed down with large stones.

If I'd had time to consider it, I wouldn't have needed the rocks for suspicion. But the confirmation... It was gut-wrenching.

And Michael, Michael whose breath was coming in sharp shudders, had risked his life in a desperate attempt to save his father. Even now, he was not yet out of danger from illness and exposure. All for a father who had never wanted to be saved.

For a long minute we stared at one another, each waiting for the other to say something. I tossed one rock as far into the murky depths as I could. I waited for Michael or Anna to argue, to stop me. No protestations came. One by one I threw the remaining rocks into the frigid waters—tossed away the evidence.

Throughout this, my boots embedded themselves deeper and deeper into the mire of the bank. When I turned to pull myself up, I slipped. I collapsed face-first in the muck. Once I managed to free myself, I registered the hysterical cackling coming from Michael. Anna and I looked to one another, desperate for some course of action.

After a few moments, with no intervention from either of us, he quieted and allowed himself to be led back to the house.

I WOULD NEVER KNOW how we managed the moments, hours, and days that followed. There was the immediate scolding from Mrs. Hudson for abandoning a tray of tarts in the oven. She trailed off mid word at the sight of us.

The scurry of footmen rushing to gather the viscount's body from the lake came next. Then the fluttering of maids, directed to fill lukewarm tubs for both Michael and myself. The kitchen was the kind of chaos that not even Mrs. Hudson could manage.

With no alternative plan, the viscount was placed on the table. Mary's feet collapsed from under her at the sight in an entirely unhelpful swoon. One of the buckets to fill the tubs was dropped all over the floor, causing others to slip in their rush back and forth. No one had seen fit to alert the butler, Weston, in the absence of a specific direction to do so. He stomped into the midst of the turmoil, complaining loudly about missing staff only to find a corpse on the table. Anna was on her knees before Michael, fretting over his silent, shivering form. She managed to move him to a chair away from the table when the viscount was brought in, but it didn't stop the empty-eyed staring. My livery was still covered top to bottom in stinking muck. And for the first time in my memory, the entire place smelled of burned pastry.

Weston, fretting tastelessly over the duty of informing the viscountess, was little help in controlling the chaos. A fair and congenial man he may have been, but he wasn't built for a crisis.

"I'll do it." The croaked words sliced the disarray. Michael had risen and tossed aside the blanket in spite of Anna's best efforts. "Let me clean up, and I'll tell her. It should be me."

"Michael, you need to warm up. You'll catch your death. And you may have frostbite!" Anna's concern seemed to shake a bit of consciousness into him.

"I'm alright."

Anna was poised to argue with him but seemed to think better of it. She sat back on her haunches when he strode purposely toward his room and waiting bath. The silence that had befallen the room at his pronouncement lingered. No one was quite certain what to do.

Finally, I could endure it no longer. "Can someone bring me something to wipe off with? I don't want to track this filth through the house." I gestured to my body.

It was Anna who eventually produced a towel and began to wipe the mud from my face with moderate success and then from the rest of me with less. With time and effort, I was clean enough to make it to Michael's vacated seat and remove my ruined boots.

As I set off for my own tub, I heard Anna take over, directing the footmen to place the viscount in a more dignified position and the maids to clean the spilled water and fetch the smelling salts for Mary.

Seven

I DIDN'T KNOW how Michael managed the conversation with Agatha. He never once spoke of it. I was there for the aftermath, though. When the tear-stricken viscountess visited her husband. His appearance was more dignified with a cloth covering both the table and his form. The kitchen, too, was dry and calm.

There was little I admired about Agatha, but in the weeks that followed, she demonstrated both a genuine love for her husband and great care for her two young sons.

That she showed no such consideration for her stepson was less praiseworthy. No words could adequately describe the vitriol she flung at him. Venom poured from her lips and hatred from her every expression.

Even in the face of the cruelty, Michael stepped in where needed. In the days and weeks after the viscount's death, he somehow became acting viscount. He set forth making necessary preparations for the service, managing the day-to-day running of the estate, and settling travel arrangements for Hugh, the new viscount, to travel from Eton.

During those dark days, he ate little and slept even less. Anna and I traded off the duty of caring for him, each trying in our own way to keep him alive when he seemed determined to work himself into a grave next to his father. We learned quickly to manage him. Too much interference from one of us resulted in a truly spectacular telling off. His patience was doubled by alternating pesterers.

He holed himself up in the viscount's study, barricaded behind a fortress of cold teacups and stale biscuits. Each plate was piled high as he took one or two sips before setting the tea aside and forgetting about it. The Judge's biscuits Anna made received similar treatment. In ordinary circumstances, I would have scolded him for his wastefulness, but I chose to ignore it in his time of mourning.

Without really meaning to, Michael became viscount in all but title. At one and ten, Hugh was hardly prepared for the duties. Agatha should have been able to manage, but she was even less qualified.

With that addition of those duties, a path emerged that neither of us saw coming.

Late into the night, or perhaps early in the morning, some weeks later, Michael finally broke.

"It's all gone," he said. He took another deep swig of the late viscount's good port. "He lost it all."

"Are you certain?"

"I've never been more certain about anything. We're fucked. He spent every last shilling. And then he spent a few thousand pounds more." He spoke with the nonchalance of a man suggesting the possibility of rain. Too exhausted to exhibit any real feeling over the subject.

"I don't suppose we're missing a ledger that's in the London house, perhaps?"

"I doubt it. But we might as well go see. The situation can hardly be worse. Besides, I ought to talk to the solicitor about this mess," he said. He flipped the ledger closed with two fingers and a great deal of irritation.

IT WAS WORSE.

Michael and I left for Grayson House a few days later. Armed with a picnic basket that Anna had packed, we set off from Kent.

I found him in the study several hours after our arrival, impressively drunk for the amount of time he had to become so. He had forgone a glass entirely, taking heavy pulls from a bottle of some amber liquid or other.

Bravely, I approached him. "I miss Anna. She knows how to deal with you when you're soused."

"You miss Anna because you think her hair is pretty, and she smells of pastry."

He wasn't wrong. I generally used more words when thinking of her and mentioned her kind heart and incredible talent. But I did love her hair and that she carried the smell of baked goods with her everywhere.

"I told you that in confidence."

"Well, I'm soused. You can't trust a soused man to keep a confidence."

"How bad is it?"

"Worse for coming here. Apparently, Agatha can run up quite a bill at the modiste."

He handed me a slip of parchment, and my jaw unhinged and fell to the floor. Hundreds of pounds... A sum that was both shocking and, somehow, entirely expected. Ridiculous baubles are costly apparently.

"For those hideous things? Really? Can't you let them repossess the damned things? It would be a gift to the whole of society for them to be off the streets."

"Who would want them back after she's worn them? They smell of death and lilacs." A snort of laughter broke free. If there was a more apt description of Agatha's gowns, I didn't know it.

"I suppose not. You know you don't have to pay me, at least not right now. Room and board is plenty."

"Augie, if I don't pay you, how will you save enough to ask Anna for her hand?"

"It's not my hand she wants anyway." The words escaped in a bitter huff.

Two years of continued evidence had demonstrated that Anna's affection for Michael ran deep. I tried not to think on it. The last two months especially, I'd had little opportunity to ruminate further, busy as I was with my self-appointed task of keeping Michael alive.

"That's not true," he protested.

"Yes, it is. But I'm not arguing with you when you're soused. It's even more fruitless than when you're sober. I came to take you with me. We're going to Temple Bar."

The idea appeared in my head as the words were leaving my mouth, but as I said it, I realized it had merit. If anything would cheer him up, even slightly, it was emptying other men's pockets.

"We are?" he asked.

"We are. Grab what's left of your purse."

"What are we doing at Temple Bar?"

"You and me, Michael, we're going to hell." The seediest of gaming hells. Perfect for a man with no coin to lose. Not that I thought Michael would lose.

"I've no money to gamble."

"Then you have nothing to lose."

The following morning, he'd won enough to pay off the modiste.

Eight

THORNTON HALL, KENT - DECEMBER 24, 1805

OVER THE NEXT FEW YEARS, I saw little of Anna. Months would go by with no contact at all. Michael needed someone to help him, and that someone was me.

If the estate went bankrupt, every single member of the family I had found would lose their livelihood, including Anna. The most expedient method of gathering funds proved to be Michael's talent at the card table. And predicting races. And foreshadowing fights. The best place to partake in such activities was London. That it was far away from Agatha was certainly to its benefit as well. But away from Agatha meant away from Anna, and that was a detriment.

Still, I was by his side through it all. Once he was able to, Michael paid me handsomely for the privilege. A footman no longer, I was a bookmaker. In just under two years, he'd nearly wiped out the entirety of the debts the viscount left behind. He had plans as well, including substantial raises for the entire staff, improvements to the tenant cottages, and a new irrigation system for the fields. But there was a cost to all this progress, and it was Michael's health.

Hazard games often started after supper and went well

into the morning, hours of drink and little food. The more success he had, the more reckless he became. Eventually, he moved from Temple Bar to the silver hells of Piccadilly, the wagers increasing with the venue. He made enemies in his quest for more coin and was called out more than once. It was an exhausting endeavor, keeping the man alive and relatively well.

I worried for Anna too. It seemed the roles of both upstairs and occasional lady's maid had been foisted upon her, leaving little time for her in the kitchens with a dusting of flour on her nose. And that meant more contact with Agatha, too, which was always an unpleasant state. But I feared for the future of Anna's bakery dreams. It seemed possible that she would settle for a position she liked well enough, rather than one she loved.

At last, I was in a carriage on my way to her. In spite of Michael's whining and blustering, even he could not argue that I spend Christmas away from my father (and my Anna). He had done his damnedest to prevent it though, arriving home from the gaming hells nearly an hour after we should have been off.

Now, seated across from me in the poorly sprung, rickety hired hack, he was snoring like the devil. One particularly loud snort was the final straw. I kicked his feet off my seat, startling him awake. He looked around, confused for a moment, before commenting, "Rude."

"So was our late start."

"We'll be there in plenty of time."

"We'll miss dinner."

"Anna will save you some. She would never let you go hungry." He leaned back into the corner of the carriage, resting his head on the wall. He tugged the collar of his great coat up around his ears against the draft seeping in from the window.

"Anna will be worried about the both of us. You've given her cause to fret for no reason."

"She has every reason to fret over me. You're doing a piss-poor job of keeping me alive. I'm exhausted, and you won't even let me rest."

"You don't pay me enough to listen to the racket coming out of your mouth."

"So, there is an amount I could pay you to let me sleep? Name it." His eyes were closed once more.

"You cannot afford it."

"Send me the bill." With that dismissal, he curled further in on himself and resumed snoring shortly after.

AT LENGTH we arrived at Thornton Hall, paying the drivers handsomely. I was given a second opportunity to nudge my slumbering companion sharply with my foot—I did not kick him.

Michael stared at the imposing red bricked manor with some trepidation. At once, I felt a pang of guilt over my treatment of him in the carriage. He was returning for my sake and would suffer for it. I doubted he had let Agatha know he would be in residence. My suspicion was all but confirmed when he followed me toward the servants' entrance to the kitchens.

In spite of our late send-off, dinner was not quite finished. Before the door had shut behind us, my father enveloped me in a great embrace. My sliver of guilt returned and intensified. My father had no other family, and I hadn't been available to him as I ought. I tightened my own arms around him, smelling the fresh scents of soap and straw. At least he'd managed to get the worst of the horse smell off for Christmas Eve dinner.

"Happy Christmas, Papa."

"Happy Christmas! You've grown since I saw you last." I hadn't. I was certain of it. A sinking feeling began when I realized how little of him there was in my arms. He was losing weight, and not an insignificant amount.

"A bit," I lied. When he finally released me, I was wrapped in Mrs. Hudson's arms before I had a moment to search out Anna. Mrs. Hudson's embrace was quick and harsh, but never failed to remind me of my own mother's hugs—what scant memories I retained.

"You're too skinny, just like Michael. Why aren't you boys eating enough?"

"Not enough of your cooking, Mrs. Hudson. London is drearier for it."

"Or raspberry tarts I'd expect." Her voice was lyrical and clear behind me. *Anna.* I turned and there she was, or some facsimile of her. It was impossible, but she'd grown even more beautiful since I'd last seen her. Even with her hair pulled back harshly, a maid's cap on her head, and the unforgivably dreary dress, she knocked the breath from my lungs.

"I don't expect there are enough of your raspberry tarts in the world to put me off them. There's not a baker in the whole of London to compare." Her answering smile was a little uncertain, but I felt it, warm in my chest, all the same.

She gestured to an empty spot next to what had always been her place. I threw myself on the long bench with a shameful amount of haste.

"Take your coat, Augie?" Michael drawled wryly from behind me. I felt the flush rise, doubly so for George's stifled chuckle. I stood back up to remove it before sitting down again, inadvertently brushing an arm against Anna's sleeve in the process. The happiest of accidents. Michael, having tossed our coats onto a nearby counter, sat down across from us.

The feast was every bit as incredible as promised. With the estate in a better financial situation than it had been even a year ago, no expense was spared. Once I was full near to bursting, Anna's plum pudding made an appearance. Made over a year before, the fruit, cognac, and port had melded into an exceptional treat. Anna thoughtfully gave me the largest serving without a word. I devoured every bite and still looked askance at the crumbs remaining on the plate.

At length, the dinner broke apart with everyone seeing to their duties, leaving Michael and me to watch unhelpfully from the table. They were kind enough to leave the spiced wine to our care, for which we were more than grateful.

Nine

THORNTON HALL, KENT - DECEMBER 25, 1805

AN HOUR OR SO LATER, the kitchen fires burned low, the dishes were all cleaned and put away, and Anna returned. I'd long since discarded my waistcoat and rolled my sleeves up my forearms indelicately. Michael had made a stealthy escape to his rooms a few moments prior while Agatha and Hugh were otherwise occupied. I only hoped his snoring didn't give him away.

I'd abandoned the bench for a seat on top of the table. Weston and Mrs. Hudson would not have approved, but they were long gone to bed. With a small hop, Anna made herself at home beside me, both of us staring into the embers of the hearth. Wordlessly, she held out a hand for the bottle I had made my own.

We sat in companionable silence for a long while, exchanging sips. I observed her with sidelong, surreptitious glances. After months of missing her, I could hardly be expected to sit beside her without looking my fill. Her hair, now free from pins and cap, adopted the deep orange of the firelight, flickering alongside it. At nineteen, the same as me, she was a woman grown with all that entailed. Her form was light, gently curved. Gone were the days of adolescence where she towered over me by several inches. Instead, she sat a mere inch or two shorter than me, the perfect height for kissing.

Eventually she broke the quiet. "So, how are you, Augie?"

I contemplated the question for a moment. As much as I missed her, and my father, I rather enjoyed my life in London. Even chasing after Michael in order to nag him. Almost immediately after his father's death, he began to look to me for advice and gave it serious consideration. It was a more impressive lot in life than I'd dreamed of as a stable master's son.

Finally, I settled on a response. "Good. Good, I think. I miss you all something terrible." A white lie; I missed her desperately. Father and occasionally Mrs. Hudson as well. Everyone else was superfluous. "But it's a greater life than I thought to lead. I don't have big dreams, not like you."

"My dreams aren't so big, not anymore."

"What do you mean?"

"Just, the bakery is getting further and further away. I don't mind this work, even for Agatha. I'm quite good as a lady's maid, and I can make a more than decent living for the right family." Before I could utter more than my sputtering wordless protest, she continued. "It will take me years to earn enough, if I ever manage. Even with Michael increasing our wages. And if I want to wed someday—which I do—I would require a husband who took no issue with his wife working day and night, leaving any children to be cared for by someone else. A man who had no issue with his wife spending relentlessly without profit, possibly for years."

"The right man wouldn't mind. He'd care more about you than the particulars of how your house is run." I bit my tongue, biting back the flood of promises. *I wouldn't mind. I love you all the more for your dreams. I want them desperately for you.*

She eyed me contemplatively. Apparently deciding to

move on from the tumultuous waters of future husbands, she said, "I have a present for you."

That sent a jolt through me. "I forgot I brought you something too. Just wait here a moment, it's in my trunk…"

She caught my bare forearm in her hand, locking me in place. For a moment we both stared at her hand on my arm before meeting each other's gaze. She released me slowly, and I felt the loss keenly.

"Me first." She hopped off the table, making an effort to avoid brushing against me once more. She went to a pantry and began to remove containers of flour, sugar, and the like. Then, at the very back, hidden from wandering hands, was a container of raspberry tarts. Carefully, she replaced the ingredients she'd displaced before bringing the tarts back to the table. A small part of me feared she would set them between us, creating distance, but she handed them to me and popped herself back on the table by my side once again.

"Anna… You have no idea how much I've missed these."

"More than me, I expect."

"Yes, I played the long game. Befriended the little slip of a girl with sunset hair all covered in flour. One day, some fifteen years later, I knew she would make me my own entire batch of raspberry tarts for Christmas."

"You're always five steps ahead of everyone else, Augie. I wouldn't put it past you."

"Well, now my gift is going to seem self-serving."

I set the tarts reverently aside before heading over to my trunk, still left by the door as I hadn't seen fit to deal with it yet. Inside, near the top, was the dusky lavender fabric-wrapped box I had agonizingly selected. On top sat a delicately embroidered Dahlia, sunset-colored like her. Inside were the spices I cased the city for. I spent months curating the selection, checking the docks for new arrivals almost daily.

When I rejoined her at the table, I handed my bounty over

gently. She ran an elegant hand over the flower, appreciating the work, before opening it. All she'd managed was a gasp of my name before I could remain silent no longer.

"I don't know how most of them are used. I hadn't even heard of half of them. But I'm certain at least a few will be of use. If you let me know which ones you like, I can make sure to get more." I could feel the rush to explain growing even stronger the longer she stared at the box in silence.

"Augustus Ainsley, this had to cost a fortune."

"Michael pays me now, less than I deserve for keeping him alive, but still better than a footman's wages. Besides—it's entirely selfish—I plan to eat whatever you make with them."

Hoping to distract her from the conversation of cost, I pried open the container at my side. The scent of caramelized pastry and ripe berries wafted up from inside. I closed my eyes to appreciate the decadent odor for a moment before selecting one carefully.

It was like biting into my childhood. Every beautiful second in this kitchen with her. Layers, both flakey and tender, melted on my tongue, balancing the tart sweetness of the raspberry jam. I could not have held back my appreciative moan for the world.

"Anna... these are somehow exactly as I remember and better than I dreamed at the same time."

"You... dreamed of my tarts?"

"Usually, you're with the tarts." It took a few seconds, distracted as I was with the decadence in my hand and in my mouth, to recognize what had spilled forth from my traitorous lips. One tart and I spilled all my secrets.

"Oh good, I would hate to be absent." Her tone was teasing, and I felt muscles I hadn't noticed tense, then relax.

I could manage this, teasing, bordering on flirtation. I could give as good as I got. I just had to watch the unspoken line. The one that developed sometime between ten and fourteen, around the time I began to notice more than her hair and her eyes. "That would be a tragedy. Fortunately for me, you're always there with the baked goods."

"What am I doing with the baked goods?" She caught my gaze then and refused to let go.

Feeding them to me. In bed. Wearing nothing but a smile. Too far—back to less fraught territory. "Making mountains of them."

"I don't think so."

"No, it's true. I eat them until I'm fat and happy. Then I keep eating until I explode." I think I had that dream... once.

She tucked a delicate curl behind her ear before shifting her weight to a hand behind her, closing the distance. Her lips were barely parted, her breath coming in soft pants against my own. When I'd turned farther toward her, I didn't know. With a trembling hand, I reached out to brush a non-existent eyelash from her cheek with my thumb—a flimsy excuse.

Her skin was so delicate, like the finest porcelain. She offered no objection, so I pressed forward, sliding my thumb along the crease of her jaw. My forefinger gently traced the line of her crooked ear. It was the only exception I'd noticed to her perfection, and I loved it all the more for its impertinence.

The remaining fingers I curled around, back to where her head and neck meet. Heart pounding in my throat, I watched her dark lashes flutter shut, gray-green eyes now hidden from mine. I leaned, ever closer, gently angling her the way I wanted her. She went willingly, eagerly.

A breath away from her lips on mine... *Crash*! The servants' door flew open, slamming into the wall next to it. We broke apart hastily as George and a newer footman swaggered in with the confidence of men who'd had far too much to drink. George quickly set his eyes on the tarts, moving to take one. I slapped his hand away, slamming the lid on my present with a glare.

Anna gathered her box, hairpins, and cap, and hopped off the table with startling efficiency. "I should be off to bed. Goodnight, Augie."

Her whispered words were small consolation for the moment lost to the two buffoons rooting through the pantry without a care in the world.

In exchange, I offered her a wry smile. "Sweet dreams, Anna." When I settled into the lumpy spare bed in the male servants' quarters, I hoped desperately that they were of me.

Ten

I HADN'T SEEN ANNA, even in passing, in more than a year. Eighteen months without a single sighting. It had been longer still, nearly six years, since that almost kiss.

The fit Agatha had thrown after discovering she had shared a roof with Michael, even for a night, was one for the records. It ensured his unwillingness to remain in the same county with her. Not even for Christmas. The irony that she hadn't even noticed his presence while he was there was apparently lost on her.

So, Anna and I were left to catch glimpses of each other in passing when Agatha was in London for the Season. Michael had earned enough in the hells by then to purchase a separate apartment, away from his stepmother's shrill protestations. We only returned to the London house for brief meetings with the young viscount. Then Hugh came of age in the winter of 1810.

Michael had an impressive windfall at the hazard table against two gentlemen of the peerage. Peers always had exponentially more money than sense. Thus, Michael declared he

49

was opening his own gaming hell. The £100,000 he earned during those twenty-eight hours was more than sufficient to fund his endeavor and set up the estate for years of success with even the barest effort.

Hugh, blissfully unaware of the true circumstances of his father's death, the previously precarious situation of the estate, or his brother's financial dealings, was less than pleased with Michael's announcement. Certain he would bring shame to the entire family, Hugh cut off his brother. Though an amusing pronouncement given the situation, it served its purpose in severing Michael from the Grayson family entirely. And severing me from my Anna.

Michael's ability to keep himself alive had improved only slightly in recent years, and it was a duty I took seriously. The idea of returning to work at the estate, now under the care of the impetuous, inexperienced viscount, was untenable. As Michael's superintendent and bookmaker, I was considered an equal and was paid well for my services. As a footman, what kind of life could I offer Anna? Had I known that our separation would appear to be rather permanent, I would have considered the choice more carefully.

Now, though, I held a letter, written in her delicate hand. Until I saw it, I had no idea the combination of elation and dread was possible, let alone so potent. Much as my heart thrilled at the sight of it, I knew there could be only one reason she was writing. I barricaded myself in my office at Wayland's, Michael's club. I needed privacy for the news I was to receive. Careful to preserve the words within, I broke the seal with uneasy hands.

October 17, 1811

My dearest Augie,

I wish I were writing to you under better circumstances. I am under the strictest instructions from your father not to interrupt your important work. But I fancy you and I have enough of an understanding that you would wish to be kept informed.

As you no doubt know, your father has been unwell for some time. He refuses all attempts to call for a doctor on his behalf, so it is difficult to know for certain, but I believe he may not be with us for much longer. His illness has spread to his lungs, and breathing seems to be a difficulty. Mother and I have endeavored to keep him as comfortable as possible.

I do not know the details of your situation at present. If there is anything you wish for me to let him know on your behalf, please send word. I will leave a candle burning for you should you wish to make the journey yourself.

Yours,
Anna

I released a shaky breath. There was still time. At least, as of two days ago. She'd sent the letter by express, but it had been delayed by the storms yesterday.

With little thought and even less delicacy, I barged into Michael's office, next to my own.

"Why do you despise knocking so, Augie?" He didn't glance up from his ledgers.

"Michael..." My voice was hoarse. I hadn't expected that.

His head popped up in alarm. He shoved his chair back and made his way around the desk to me without a word. I'd forgotten the letter, still in my hand, until he gently pried it from my grasp. After skimming the short missive quickly, he made no comment. Instead, he rang for a servant before setting the letter carefully on the edge of his desk. Still in silence, he poured two glasses of my favorite whiskey, handing me one and leading me to one of the armchairs in front of his desk.

Swallowing was difficult; not for the burn, but for the knot that had made its home in my throat. I had made little progress in my drink when one of the footmen entered with a solicitous knock—Potter, I think was his name. Still not sure of his purpose, I took another sip.

"Potter, I need you to head next door and pack a trunk for both Augie and myself. We'll need provisions for at least a week. Ask Baldwin to have the carriage readied. Augie and I will be leaving within the hour, if possible. Let Baldwin know, once he calls for the carriage, he is to close the club until our return. Anyone currently playing may cash out now or have their game paused until we reopen. Their drinks are on us, and offer them £50 for a future visit. Have a sign placed on the door saying we are closed for the next several days. Do you understand?"

I could do nothing more than stare in awe at Michael. I hadn't considered he would join me. At once, I recognized the sentiment for the uncharitable thought it was. Though Michael was careless with his own health and happiness, he had never been anything other than a generous friend to me.

Potter struggled to repeat the instructions. A good man he may be, but intelligent he was not. With a sigh, Michael told him to send Baldwin up and go pack our trunks, not giving him the opportunity for miscommunication. Moments later, Baldwin arrived with a notepad. I knew I liked him for a reason. As requested, within the hour Michael and I were on the road to Kent.

Eleven

THORNTON HALL, KENT - OCTOBER 19, 1811

THE CARRIAGE MOVED SWIFTLY. The driver pressed the horses faster than I would have in his place. Still, every mile felt an eternity. Sitting in a carriage, doing nothing, helping no one —it was excruciating. The first quarter hour of the ride was for planning. Michael would find an inn at Margate after dropping me off and then return. I would stay with my father—if there was time.

Every few minutes, Michael peered up at me from the ledgers he was pretending to study, waiting for some kind of reaction, I supposed. I was waiting for it as well. I was hanging, suspended. My father was alive until I determined otherwise, yet he was dead until I received proof of life. It was a kind of torture I hadn't known before.

When Mama died, I had been by her side. When the viscount died, I helped pull his body from the water. Both situations were horrible in different ways, but this... this was worse somehow. Not knowing might actually kill me.

I felt my absence over the last few years more keenly than ever before. I always intended to visit—next week or next month, perhaps. Then before I realized it, years had passed.

54

Years I hadn't spent with my father; years he had been struggling or in pain, and I hadn't been by his side to help. The thought left a sour taste in my mouth and a tumultuous flip in my stomach.

Finally, as we neared the great house, we slowed slightly, and the stable appeared, my father's cottage not far beyond them. Before the carriage had completed its halting shutter, I was clambering out.

The cottage was worn down. In my youth, my father had prided himself on its appearance. To see it missing shingles with cracked windowpanes was heart-wrenching. At the threshold, I froze. As untenable as my present state of ignorance was... I had been wrong before. Certainly, it was better than knowing the worst.

I felt a hand on my shoulder, warm and firm. Michael. "Do you want me to go in first?"

"No, I..." My choice was taken from me as the heavy door creaked open. And there she was. Anna. Disheveled and clearly exhausted, but warm and real and as beautiful as ever.

"Augie! You made it! I feared the storms would wash out the road, and you wouldn't get here in time."

"So I am? In time?"

"Yes, but only just, I'm afraid. He's stopped eating the other day, and I'm hardly able to coax him to drink."

She opened the door wider, gesturing us inside. The cottage was in worse repair inside. And the smell... Anna was right. It did smell of sickness and death. I heard a rasping, racking cough from the bedroom. Michael and Anna hung back as I approached, giving me a moment.

He was doubled over the side of the bed, desperately hacking, trying to remove whatever was in his lungs, clearly failing.

Unsure, I knocked on the doorframe, alerting him to my presence. Between coughs, he tried to roll himself back onto the bed. Without thought, I was at his side, helping him sit back. Once settled, he opened his eyes and saw me. "Augie! What are you doing here?"

"I'm here to visit you, Papa."

"I hope Anna didn't send for you. She's been hovering something fierce. I keep telling her I'll be right as rain once I cough up whatever it is."

"I'm sure you will be. I had a few days off and thought I would come visit my favorite person."

"Anna?"

A feminine chuckle came from the doorway and in spite of everything, I felt a small smile tugging at the corners of my mouth.

"You, Papa."

"Liar. My hair, what's left of it, isn't nearly so pretty."

That earned a chuckle from me. That surprised me a bit. I hadn't thought I was capable of it at the moment.

"You're not wrong. She did say you weren't eating or drinking."

"She likes to fuss. I'm fine."

"I think I'd like some tea. It's rather chilly outside. Would you take some with me?"

"If you're already making some. I don't want to be any bother."

"Well, I am."

I left him to his own devices for a moment, moving back into the main room. Anna was already putting the kettle on the fire.

Michael pulled me aside. "Are you alright? I'll be back with the carriage shortly."

"Yes, thank you."

"No thanks necessary." With that he was off, back in the carriage headed toward Margate.

"I'm glad you came." Anna's voice was quiet, barely

audible really. She was seated at the small round table in the center of the room.

Before I could respond, the coughing resumed from the next room. He could barely draw breath before the next wave hit. It was a wonder he hadn't broken a rib. I moved to go help him, to comfort him somehow.

"Don't. He prefers to do that bit alone. A last bit of dignity, I think. You can't help anyway."

Every instinct in me as a son fought against it. But I forced myself to sit across from her at the table, listening helplessly to the wretched, barking coughs in the next room.

As soon as I collapsed in the chair, the fight left me. Whatever was holding me upright disappeared in a great rush. Without energy, I dropped my heavy head into my arms on the table. I heard a chair scratch the floor, then a soft, pastry-scented hand rested on my shoulder. Anna's soft presence beside me was more fortifying than any tea or spirit. I rolled my head to face her.

"Thank you. I cannot ever thank you enough, Anna. For everything you've done. For writing to me. I just... Thank you."

"You don't have to thank me. I want to be here. Your father is a good man who raised one himself. I am glad to be able to help him now. I only wish I could be of actual help."

I sat up, catching her gaze with mine.

"You are, more than you know. For both of us." The unmistakable sounds of a bubbling kettle interrupted our stare. She pushed the chair back, busying herself with tea preparations.

"I haven't been able to get any laudanum into him. He refuses. I suppose putting some in his tea is very wrong, isn't it?" She peered at me with a guilty, questioning expression.

Another racking cough pierced through the room, this time accompanied by choking sounds on inhale.

"Do it, just a bit. I'll try to get him to take a full dose tonight." She nodded, measuring a small dose. Hopefully enough to ease his pain slightly.

"Do you need to get back to the house?"

"Mary and Martha are covering my duties."

"Martha?"

"She's new. There are a few since you were last here. And we've lost some as well. George moved on. Did you know Philip? He's gone too. We can discuss the estate later. He's quieted some. See if he'll take the tea.

With more grace than any one person should possess, she lifted the tray, laden with tea and a few sandwiches, before I could take it from her. Through some sort of witchcraft, she opened the door with both hands occupied and settled the tray on the side table.

Handing the doctored cup to my father, she said, "I expect you to enjoy at least a cup, Mr. Ainsley. I went through all the trouble to make it."

He took a sheepish sip. She'd learned the trick to manipulating my father. "You too," she directed me with a wink, closing the door behind her.

I settled on the chair by the bed, taking my own cup in hand. I wasn't particularly thirsty, but if my efforts would help my father at all, I would do far more.

"I hope you're prepared for that woman. She'll keep you on your toes."

"I've been preparing my entire life, but she's not mine, Pa."

"Tell that to her. She don't have any other sweethearts. I keep an eye for 'em and scare 'em off for you." I chuckled my thanks for his efforts. "She's not going to wait forever, though. Best get her wed and bedded."

"Papa!"

"What? I've watched you stare at that girl since you were four years old. She's waited plenty long."

"I'm not talking about this."

"All right, but just remember what I said. The good ones don't wait forever. And if you get one, you may not have as long with her as you want, so you best get to it." My heart tugged at the memory of Mama and the thought of how little time my father had with her.

He was seized with another burst of coughs. This time I rubbed his back through the hacks. Anna was right. It seemed to offer little comfort. At length, he settled once more.

"Tell me about the trouble you and Michael get up to in town."

"What do you want to know?"

"Everything."

"Well, you just missed Michael's black eye. Part of the club is under construction, and he walked right into an open beam."

"I'd laugh at him, but my chest hurts too much to laugh just now."

"That's quite all right. I laughed at him more than enough for the both of us."

"What else?"

HIS TEA SEEMED to help with Papa's cough a little. My voice grew hoarse with storytelling, and he grew more and more quiet. Eventually, he kept his eyes closed, offering little hand movements to indicate when I should go on. Eventually, I forced myself to say the words that had been on the tip of my tongue for hours. "Do you want some laudanum, Papa? Just to help you sleep."

When he wheezed out, "All right, thank you," I knew.

I measured a more than generous dose and helped him sit up to drink it.

"I love you, Papa."

"I love you. Do you have any more stories to make me proud with?"

"Yes, of course. How about the time I won £300 off an earl?" He nodded, so I told him about the Earl of Westfield, whose misfortunes were my fortunes. He fell asleep shortly after, but I continued, story after story, long after some part of me knew he was gone. I couldn't bring myself to stop talking, to stop giving him reasons to be proud.

I don't know how long I sat there, babbling about nothing, tears in my eyes and my heart in my throat. At some point, Anna came in and sat next to me, taking the hand that wasn't holding my father's cold one. Michael followed and took the other side of the bed for his own silent vigil.

It was only after I ran out of stories that the tears broke free. Deep, racking sobs to rival my father's coughs. I found my face pressed to Anna's lap, her hands running soothingly through my hair. I would never remember making my way to my old bedroom and falling asleep.

Twelve

GRAYSON HOUSE, LONDON - JANUARY 12, 1814

NEARLY THREE YEARS passed before the opportunity arose to see Anna again, and it came from a most unexpected corner.

I had spent hours combing through the records of one of our regulars, Richard Dalton, the Earl of Westfield. He was wagering with money he didn't have. Funds he had no hope of repaying in the event of a loss. Which meant he wasn't intending to lose.

But wagering such a sum on a match so heavily favored one way... There was every chance he'd paid off Johnson, the favorite boxer. Of course, informing Michael was almost enough of a headache that I should count the money a wash and be done with it. But I disliked Westfield. And I was far too good at my job to ignore such an obvious scheme.

"I assume you've already located Johnson?" Michael asked after I shared my suspicions.

"Of course."

"Why is my name on the building and not yours, Augie?" A question I'd pondered often myself.

"I've no idea, but the carriage is ready for you."

"Humble as always, Augie."

We continued back and forth for some time, debating the likelihood and severity of Michael's imminent beating. Accusing such a skilled fighter of throwing a match wasn't likely to end well for Michael.

"Wonderful. After Johnson is finished physically beating me within an inch of my life, I'm to dine at Grayson House tonight. Agatha can handle the emotional torture." At the words Grayson House, I felt my heart skip—Anna.

Pressing him for more information, I continued, "Why on earth are you dining there?"

"I received an invitation this morning. Apparently, Hugh's new wife comes from some sort of happy family. Whatever that is. She seems to think forced proximity is sufficient to encourage familial congeniality."

Hugh was married? That was an unexpected development. I had thought he would wait until he was nearly thirty before choosing a wife.

Michael's complaints about happy families were nearly all bluster. He'd grown up with the same family I had. We sat in the kitchens in Thornton Hall every night enjoying Mrs. Hudson's cooking and Anna's baking.

"And you're sure she meant to invite you? Not Tom?"

"Tom will be there too."

"At least you'll have one ally."

"I was hoping for two." There it was. The chances of Anna being in town were slim, and even Mrs. Hudson's cooking wasn't enough for me to risk Agatha's wrath, not without the promise of Anna.

"No, absolutely not."

"Augie..."

"No. Besides, someone needs to watch the play if you're dining out." That wasn't strictly true. Baldwin could manage the card play in our absence as he'd proven invaluable time and again. But it served as a handy excuse.

"I'm given to understand that Anna has taken over as lady's maid for the new viscountess... I'm certain her hair is still pretty and she retains that pastry scent you find so alluring." The linchpin. The one word with guaranteed results. *Anna.*

And so it was decided, we were both headed to Grayson House this evening.

~

IT WAS NEARLY SEVEN. We were almost certain to be late given the slush accumulating on the road. It was entirely Michael's fault. While I had dressed with more care than I usually—ever—showed, I had done so efficiently. His Johnson-swollen eye might have been a slight distraction, but that was hardly an excuse to be late to dinner.

Finally, the carriage shuddered to a halt, and the driver signaled our arrival. Michael stepped out and immediately stopped in front of the steps. I was left trapped, half out of the carriage. He stared at the door as though it might bite him. I suppose, though the door would not, the occupants might. His fears were a little founded.

"Are you going in the front or the back?" I asked.

"I suppose I should knock. Did we determine a distress signal?"

Oh no, I did not agree to act as rescuer. I hadn't set eyes on Anna in years. I wouldn't be distracted by Michael's new sister-in-law's delusions.

"We did not, and I won't be rescuing you. I will be wooing Anna with my handsome countenance and vast wealth. You're not to interrupt. You might distract her with *your* wealth and countenance."

That was the thick of it. I was finally in a position to woo Anna. To be the man that she deserved. My hard-earned confidence wasn't so impressive that I was willing to risk Michael impressing her in my stead.

"That seems unlikely, but I wish you the best of luck. Two quick rings of the bell followed by two slow then?"

"I'll leave you to rot." Probably.

"Good luck with your wooing. Don't forget to invite me to the wedding." His invitation was entirely dependent on whether he interrupted my efforts tonight.

Down the alleyway, I found the servants' entrance. Faced with my own door, I was now every bit as useless as Michael. Eventually, I gathered enough courage to knock. The door burst open, and I was wrapped in Mrs. Hudson's arms before words could escape me.

"Oh, I'm so glad you came! You've grown too!" As quickly as she had yanked me into her arms, she pushed me back by my shoulders just as fast. "And look at you, so handsome!"

I was still trying to extricate myself from the inspection when I heard a delicate giggle behind her.

There she was. Anna stood leaning a shoulder confidently against the opposite door, her other hand lazily resting on her hip. The air abandoned my lungs for places unknown.

Even in a dowdy maid's uniform she was the picture of loveliness. She had forgone the cap, and her hair was escaping its pins in loose curls. They were kissed by the firelight the way the sunset kissed the clouds. A bright red flash in the sky. It had darkened slightly, reminding me more of the last glimpse before twilight than the first brushes of sunset that it resembled in our youth. Still, every bit as stunning as the first time.

Except she was a woman grown now, in form and countenance. She carried herself in the manner of a woman who knew exactly what she had done to me and was quite proud of the result. She deserved to be proud. I hadn't been struck speechless at the sight of a woman since I was four years old. And she was a girl then.

"Hello, Augie." Her voice had deepened from my memory too, now huskier and more sensual.

I opened my mouth to respond only to realize it had been hanging open for some time. With a swallow I responded, "Hello, Anna. You're looking well."

There was a pause before she responded, performing a slow perusal of her own. "You as well. We're about to start supper. Please join us."

I trailed after her into the kitchen with Mrs. Hudson behind us. The table was filled with mostly new faces, but I was greeted warmly as I took my place next to Anna. If I resembled a puppy dogging his master's heels for instruction, that was fine by me as long as I was beside her.

"I was surprised Michael agreed to this dinner," she commented.

"I suspect Tom had a hand in it. So, Hugh has wed?"

"Yes, Kate. I'm her lady's maid."

"Congratulations. Are you enjoying the role?" Lord, this was stilted. I took a hearty swig of the wine in front of me.

"Yes, very much. Kate is very kind."

"How did she end up with Hugh then?"

"Augie!"

"What? He's a bit young to wed. She must be a special woman."

"Well, she is." Under her breath, Anna added, "and far too good for him." I snorted lightly into my glass of wine —charming.

"Don't fret. Agatha will berate the kindness right out of her."

"She is certainly putting forth the effort."

"Who are we talking about? Agatha and the viscountess?"

A new footman chimed in boisterously. "You should see it. Every night there's a dining room war."

"A war?"

"Agatha goes for the foot of the table—where the viscountess is supposed to sit. The first time it happened, I just stood there with my mouth hanging open. So did her ladyship. For a woman with a megrim moments before, Agatha seemed remarkably recovered. Then she did it again the next night. And again.

"Her ladyship keeps looking to his lordship, expecting him to do something. Obviously, that wasn't going to happen. So, she took it upon herself. Agatha may be on a mission, but she's no match for a twenty-something anymore. Her ladyship all but runs to the seat to get there first. Agatha stood staring, mouth all pursed like it always is. But what is she going to do? It's not her seat, and she knows it. So now they battle it out every night. Her ladyship always wins now. We have an agreement to turn the chair in her favor."

"It's not surprising that Agatha hasn't taken to displacement well."

"Not in the slightest. She's always been difficult, but it's so much worse now. If it weren't for her ladyship, I think the entire staff would've left."

"She's taken well to the role then? I'm sorry, I missed your name."

"Jon. As well as she can with such a husband." He turned back to his companion, leaving Anna and me to our private conversation.

"She's had a rough go of it, I think. She's a vicar's daughter. I don't think she intended to be married to Hugh any more than he intended to be married. She's taken to it better than he has, though."

"Not surprising. How is everyone else? Your mother seems well, if the veracity of her embrace is any indication."

"She's right as rain. Weston is still Weston. He thinks he's in charge, but he hasn't the slightest idea. Mary is still here in spite of her best efforts to entrap a footman."

"Still?"

"Her efforts have increased."

"It doesn't seem like enough staff to run the house, not with a young viscountess. She must be entertaining."

"She does occasionally, and she's planning a ball." Her voice dropped to a near whisper, and she concentrated on her plate. "I think the estate is struggling again. Hugh is not a particularly attentive landlord."

Following her example, I focused on my own servings. "Do you want me to speak to Michael?"

"No. It's Hugh's mess now. He wouldn't accept help from Michael, even if he offered. And it wouldn't be deserved if he did."

"You'll inform me if you change your mind?"

I was forced to refill my glass from a nearby pitcher. It was warm in the kitchens, and the cool wine was refreshing.

"How have you been?" she asked.

"Well, I watched Michael receive a punch to the face today. That was enjoyable."

"Did you do the punching?"

"Tragically, no."

"I'm ever so sorry for you."

"Your sympathies are appreciated. My day-to-day work involves a great deal of paperwork. Solving problems before they happen, that sort of thing. Michael has been very successful though, so it's become quite a lot of paperwork."

"So, quite exciting then?"

"Yes, very. Do you still have time to bake?"

Her expression was both regretful and resigned. She knew I would ask, and the answer was no. I was certain of it. "Not very much, unfortunately. Not when we're so short staffed."

Supper was coming to a quick close, staff returning to evening duties one by one. My time with Anna was growing short.

"I am sorry to hear it. You seem well pleased with your position with the viscountess, though?"

"I am. But tell me more of the mysterious club. Surely, it's not all paperwork."

I had to refill my glass once more, tiny thing that it was. "Truly, that is the majority of it. Though, we do have occasional bouts of excitement to keep us invested. I discovered a marquess, who shall remain unnamed, slipping dice down his trousers. Apparently, he felt that rubbing them against his manhood would bring him luck." She fought to hold back her laughter for a moment before it burst forth. I felt ten-thousand feet tall as her head fell back with delight, her green-gray eyes crinkling.

Then I heard Michael's voice from behind me and Mrs. Hudson questioning his eye. His arrival signaled the end of the evening's entertainment to Anna. She hugged him briefly before returning to her charge.

He made the effort to slump my arm over his shoulder. I wasn't that in my cups, but I suspected he needed an occupation after an evening with Agatha. And if assuming I was quite drunk got me a night away from the club to reminisce about Anna, well that was all the better.

Thirteen

FROM THE PERSPECTIVE of the upstairs diners, the supper was by all accounts an unmitigated disaster. Apparently, this was not a deterrent to Hugh's new wife. Every week the invitation came. Every week we attended. I suspected Michael felt sympathetic toward the new viscountess and was happy to serve as Agatha's punching bag for a few hours. Or, if not strictly happy, willing.

I, on the other hand, was ecstatic.

Week after week, I learned more about the woman Anna had become in my absence. Generous, kind, witty—these were nothing new. The younger maids looked to her for inspiration, and she led with grace and compassion. She was completely unwilling to entertain my nonsense and determined to be unimpressed by me; she was more guarded. It was difficult to determine whether the new, more wary nature was due to our change in circumstances or our lack of privacy. All our interactions had been in the kitchens, tripping over others.

When I was finally graced with an afternoon off, my only thoughts were of her. My first stop was the florist. I left armed with dahlias. Though they were a pale imitation of the sunset, put to shame by the variety of colors in her hair, they were the closest match I could find.

Once I reached Grayson House, I knocked on the servants' entrance and was granted entry by one of the new footmen, who was now familiar to me, although I couldn't recall his name. I paid attention to little outside of Anna during our dinners.

"You can sit at the table if you'd like. I'll see if she has a few minutes."

"Thank you."

I made myself at home on the bench, resting my back against the table to wait. The kitchens were quiet. The day was still too early to begin dinner preparations.

As five minutes became ten, I spun around on the bench, studying the grooves in the oak table. Most were as familiar to me as the lines on my palms.

Some, though, were new. I wondered at the deep horizontal gash in front of me. There were scald marks I could only assume came from hot serving dishes. I hoped whatever they'd contained had been delicious, and worth the scar as a reminder.

As I stared, the changes became more apparent. Drawing my thumbnail back and forth in the groove in front of me, the minutes passed slowly. The occasional scullery maid scurried past, arms fully laden. But no sign of Anna.

After nearly three quarters of an hour, a feminine form slipped into the entry. Unfortunately, it wasn't the one I was waiting on.

"Oh, I'm sorry. I had no idea you were here. Are you waiting for someone?" The woman was short with dark hair and wide blue-green eyes and alabaster skin. Her dress was elegant and tasteful. There was only one person this could be: the new viscountess.

I stood quickly, the bench scraping the ground. I flushed

at the unpleasant sound before bowing. "Lady Grayson, forgive me. I would not wish to be a bother."

"You're no bother! You must be Mr. Ainsley. I've heard a great deal about you. Have you seen Mrs. Hudson by chance?" I could feel my face contorted in confusion but could do little to school it. How would she know me?

Choosing to answer her question before interrogating her, I answered, "I haven't. I expect she may be at the market."

"Oh dear. I was hoping my friend, Juliet, would stay for dinner."

"Knowing Mrs. Hudson, there will be plenty. If there's a concern, she is quite adept at stretching the meat with an abundance of vegetables." Her look of trepidation softened only slightly. "I am certain you have no cause for worry."

"Thank you. I just hate to make her work more difficult."

"She's worked for Agatha for more than two decades. It's quite impossible for you to be more difficult than her." A huff of a laugh escaped her before she covered her mouth with a flush.

"I suppose you're here to kidnap my lady's maid?"

"The thought had crossed my mind. May I ask... that is..."

"How do I know of you?"

"Well, yes."

"I've known about you since that first night. You had Anna quite distracted. And Michael talks of no one else."

"That's because he's incapable of retaining friends that he doesn't pay."

Another laugh burst forth, and she let this one free. Her face alighted with delight. I'd known her but a few minutes, and I already knew she was too good for Hugh.

"I am certain that's not true. He's been nothing but kind to me. I can see Anna's problem though." My stomach dropped.

"Her problem?"

71

"Well, you're quite charming. Handsome as well. I'm given to understand the club does quite well, so I expect you're wealthy too. Quite difficult to resist."

"I don't want her to resist!"

That earned another laugh, though this one was somewhat less charming given it was at my expense.

"I imagine you don't. But why shouldn't she? From what I understand, you've been popping in and out of her life since you were seventeen. Getting her hopes up only to dash them. Why is this time any different?"

I'd been—what? Her hopes were involved? I felt my jaw slacken as I stared at her, not really seeing. Memories of the last years flashed before me. Without warning, my weakened knees gave way, and I all but fell back on the bench.

My gaze returned to the table with all its new blisters and pockmarks. Suddenly, I saw the wounds in a new light. I knew the bones of the table, the defects and scars of old, but the new ones that had arisen in my absence... I wasn't there for them. I'd missed those stories. I wondered about the scars Anna had developed, the ones I wasn't there for.

She had helped me through the worst of mine, but she'd asked for nothing in return. Had there been moments when she'd needed or wanted me, and I hadn't been there?

"I didn't intend for you to question your entire life's trajectory."

I'd quite forgotten she was there. I was in a state.

"I'm sorry, I..."

"Don't be sorry. Just... be certain. If you want to be in her life, be in her life. If you cannot be here for her, then let her go. She hasn't said as such, but I sense that her heart breaks a little each time you leave." A lump had arisen in my throat, and my efforts to swallow it were futile.

Before I could answer, the door burst open with the flurry that was Mrs. Hudson returning from the market.

Arms burdened with bags and packages, she was trailed by Anna in a similar state. Two footmen followed, even more laden. Anna deposited her parcels without noting me, turning to direct one of the footmen before she saw me.

"Augie! What on earth are you doing here?" *I came to bring you flowers and see if you would take a walk.* Given Lady Grayson's comments, it seemed a woefully inadequate plan. I shot a look to her for help, only to discover she had disappeared entirely.

Unable to hide the slightly wilted flowers, I was forced to press on with that part of my plot at least. Made more uncomfortable by the presence of her mother and the footmen as witnesses, my speech was stilted. "I, uh, came to see you, to bring you these." Not at all the suave declaration I had seen in my mind. Especially combined with the snickering of the footmen.

She, at least, was unbothered by my unease and the mirth of our crowd. "They're lovely! Thank you, Augie!"

She turned away, searching through cabinets, presumably for a vase, while I searched for the words to convey all my feelings.

Lady Grayson returned, feigning a first arrival. "Oh good, I found you, Mrs. Hudson! Please tell me if it's any trouble. I was hoping to add one more to dinner tonight."

"Of course not, ma'am. The roast looked particularly fine today. It's more than large enough for one more."

"You're certain?"

"Not a lick of trouble to be had."

"Wonderful! Oh, excuse me, Mr.—?"

Anna jumped in. "My lady, this is Augustus Ainsley. He works with Michael and served as footman here for many years."

"Lovely! I'm glad to meet you, Mr. Ainsley. Anna, are

those flowers for you? They're beautiful!" I made a second introductory bow. Her discretion was admirable.

"Yes, Augie brought them. I was just searching for a vase."

"I think I have something that would suit them well. Would you like to use it?"

"Are you certain?"

"Oh, yes." She caught sight of Mary passing through in the corner. "Mary? Would you mind fetching that vase in my sitting room? It's on top of the desk." Mary offered a curtsy in response before heading off in search of the illustrious vase.

"Thank you!"

"No need to thank me. These are exquisite. They deserve a worthy home. You have fine taste, Mr. Ainsley. They remind me slightly of her hair." I could do little more than flush in response.

I needed to press forward. I could not leave without a plan to secure Anna's company, despite the watchful eyes of an entire household staff. Lady Grayson kindly turned her attention back toward Mrs. Hudson, giving me an opportunity.

Anna was gazing at her flowers, seemingly appreciatively. Perhaps this afternoon wouldn't be a complete disaster.

"Anna." My voice broke slightly, and I had to clear my throat. "I was hoping you might accompany me to the theater sometime at your convenience?"

Her eyes snapped to mine, rosy mouth parting slightly in surprise. She hesitated, though, and my heart was in my throat as I awaited her answer.

"The two of us?"

"With a chaperone, of course."

"I am working, though." She looked in askance toward her employer as though she wanted to attend with me. I bit back a smile. It was far from the agreement to be mine forever, which was the ultimate design.

Lady Grayson overheard. "I can certainly spare you for one

night, Anna. You've been working so hard to assist me with planning for the ball on Friday. Perhaps the night after? The fifth?" I was nodding far too eagerly, before she even offered a date.

Anna had perked up with the offer of a night off before she shrank slightly. "I don't have anything to wear." The whisper was barely audible and heartbreakingly disappointed.

Before I could offer her everything I had and beg to purchase as many gowns and bonnets and slippers and pelisses and reticles as her heart desired, Lady Grayson spoke again.

"We'll work something out, Anna. I won't have you in the theater in your uniform." It seemed that, in spite of her warnings, she was willing to assist me.

Anna still hadn't agreed, though.

"Please, Anna?"

She hesitated a moment longer before nodding and tucking a loose strand of fiery hair behind her ear. The gesture was uncertain. Uncertainty was unfamiliar on her. I wanted her to be sure of me, but I had to earn that.

"Saturday then? I will send word with the time?"

"Yes, that would be nice." I felt the relieved smile blooming. I had plans to make. Michael to coerce into running his own club. Tickets to purchase. My formerly free afternoon was filling quickly, and I couldn't be happier for it.

"Thank you, Anna."

"Thank you for the flowers, Augie. They're truly stunning."

Fourteen

MICHAEL'S... paramour, Lady Celine Hasket, Marchioness of Rycliffe, maintained a box in the Theatre Royal, Drury Lane. Always a generous woman, she had offered us the use of her box and agreed to serve as chaperone. Apparently, the Frenchwoman was a close friend of the viscountess as well.

As luck would have it, the theater was performing a Shakespearean comedy and not one of the tragedies. I didn't think a tragedy would set the right tone for our outing.

Until this morning, time had dragged. Today, however, it had moved so quickly, I hardly knew what to do with myself. Michael had been no help at all. He was off apologizing for a series of blunders he had caused at Kate's ball the night before.

Arriving late with a blackened eye hadn't impressed his new sister. He had been successful in his efforts to corner Westfield, however. Unfortunately, the man's daughter learned of her dowry's fate and her sham engagement by eavesdropping. It was a less-than-ideal circumstance.

Beside me in the carriage, I had another bouquet filled to the brim with dahlia's, tulips, and roses in varying shades of yellow, orange, red, and pinks. This time I included a vase with them. I may have been a dolt on occasion, but I learned from my errors.

I wore my finest greatcoat and trousers. Everything was brushed and shined to perfection. I even had my hair trimmed for the occasion. Still, with all the preparations, I felt the urge to fuss with my waistcoat. I had donned and doffed my hat repeatedly on the short drive.

Lady Rycliffe was atypically quiet across from me, and, in my nerves, I was a less-than-impressive conversationalist myself. She wore a deep amethyst gown that was, as usual, stunning in its lack of adornment. Physically, Lady Rycliffe was tiny in every way. Short and rail thin, she always managed to tailor any gown in the latest fashion plates to fit her form perfectly. Her golden curls elegantly swept from her neck. She rejected the latest hair fashions in favor of a more simplistic style that suited her more.

Lady Rycliffe was a frequent visitor to the club. Though women weren't strictly permitted, gentlewomen anyway, fashionable widows of consequence were often an exception. Lady Rycliffe was a favorite: charming, beautiful, and perfectly content to set down any man who got out of hand. She had the confidence of a woman who had loved and lost and had no time to suffer fools. She captivated the *ton*. I often wondered why she tolerated Michael.

Far before I was ready, the carriage pulled up to Grayson House and halted with a shudder. My legs made no effort to cooperate with my thoughts. Instead, I stared at the house with trepidation.

"Augie, you are ready. She will adore the evening. Now, let us go fetch your future bride, *oui*?"

With a deep breath, I replied, "*Oui*."

"*Bien*. Now, you must exit so you may assist me out of the carriage." Her instructions should have been unnecessary, but I was thankful for them. She was also kind enough to knock on the imposing front door. More than twenty years I had lived in one of the Grayson estates, and I could count on one finger the number of times I used that door. Left to my own devices, I probably would have escorted a lady of the peerage down the alleyway and into the kitchens out of sheer habit.

Weston greeted Lady Rycliffe with alacrity and me with a knowing smirk, ushering us into the drawing room. On the short trek, I saw no fewer than four servants peering with interest from behind partially closed doors and around corners.

Our wait was no more than a few minutes before the viscountess entered, greeting Lady Rycliffe warmly.

"Anna will be down in a moment," she informed me. I nodded and was left to shift my balance from foot to foot uneasily, too nervous to sit. Catching sight of the floral arrangement on the mantel, I remembered my own with alarm, abandoned on the seat in the carriage.

"I forgot something in the carriage, I'll be right—" and there she was. Anna, such as I had never seen her. The sunlight streamed through the large windows of the drawing room, framing her in the golden glow. Instead of her usual uniform, she wore a sage gown with lace overtop. The sleeves were short and matching gloves went past her elbows. The dress was cut low, lower than I'd ever seen on her, emphasizing her tall, elegant frame in a way that was entirely unnecessary but entirely appreciated.

Shades of auburn, burgundy, copper, and mahogany weaved through her hair, adorned with a simple sage ribbon. Her cheeks were flushed a bit more deeply than I was used to, and her lips a berry pink. Most distracting of all, though, were her eyes. They were more green than gray in the sunset, and the coloring of the gown drew more attention to them. Framed by thick, black lashes, the tips of which shone red in the glow of the window.

She was Anna, but more. She always carried herself with confidence, but there was a sensuality now. She seemed to feel beautiful, and it made her all the more alluring.

"Augie?" At her quiet question, I blinked, clearing my mind. I had been staring for far longer than was appropriate, and I wasn't entirely certain there wasn't drool hanging from my slack jaw. "What did you forget?"

"Oh, blast! I brought you flowers, but I've left them in the carriage. I'll be right back." I moved to pass her, to retrieve the flowers, but she caught my upper arm in her gloved grasp.

"You just brought me flowers! You didn't need to bring more. Weston can get them, though. You don't mind, do you?"

I had quite forgotten there were other people in the world, let alone in the room. Weston's smirk had grown even further, but I couldn't bring myself to care. Frankly, the fact that everyone else in the room wasn't having the same reaction indicated their poor taste rather than anything I should feel shame over. One doesn't stand in the presence of an angel and continue chatting about gowns like Lady Rycliffe and her friend were. Weston agreed to fetch the arrangement.

Anna glanced down at her feet. I caught sight of tiny ivory slippers under the hem of her gown. "You look very fine, Augie."

"Oh, yes. I mean, you as well. I... You're breathtaking, Anna."

"Thank you. It's the finest thing I've ever worn."

"You've been taking my breath away since you were four years old. You don't need the dress." I hadn't intended to say that, but her pleased flush made me glad I had. Weston returned with the arrangement, earning me Anna's gasp of approval.

"Augie, this is too much." She danced a gloved finger over

the petals in the crystal vase in Weston's hands. "Thank you," she addressed me, sincerity in her tone and eyes.

"They're lovely. I'll have them sent to your room, Anna?" Kate asked.

"Yes, thank you."

"You three had best be off if you want to see the beginning."

Beside the viscountess, Lady Rycliffe rolled her eyes slightly. We'd had an in-depth discussion about the importance of arriving fashionably late. I insisted that Anna had never been, and she was going to see the entire thing if she wished, fashion be damned. At length, Lady Rycliffe had relented with an indulgent smile.

I offered Anna my arm, and she slipped hers through, tucking herself close to me. We paused at the entry to retrieve her and Lady Rycliffe wraps and my greatcoat.

Once inside the dimly lit carriage, Lady Rycliffe slid to one side to allow Anna to sit across from me.

"So, Augie, are you going to introduce me to your guest?" she asked with an amused grin.

"Apologies. Anna, this is Lady Celine Hasket, Marchioness of Rycliffe."

"I jest. We met when I last visited Kate. I must say, the gown becomes you, Anna. I will be fending off suitors from every box in the theater on your behalf tonight. Everyone will wish to make the acquaintance of *la belle femme en vert.*"

"But I'm only a maid..."

"And a beautiful woman." I could do little more than glare at Lady Rycliffe. "Relax, Augustus, I have no intention of offering her to the highest bidder. And I have no doubt you would outbid them all if I did."

My continued glare was interrupted by Anna's quiet, "I don't want to meet anyone but Augie."

My gaze returned once more to the beauty before me. She

smiled softly in my direction. Then I felt a tiny nudge against the instep of my shoes. A delicate cream slipper pressed against mine from beneath the hem of her gown.

My heart flipped for a beat before I recovered, trapping her foot between my own, keeping her close. When we arrived, the lineup to the theater was not long, much to Lady Rycliffe frustration about our early arrival. There was a great deal of muttering in French. My grasp of the language was limited, but I caught one or two words that were indelicate at best.

"Thank you for arriving early, Lady Rycliffe."

"You should be grateful. I will have to hide in the retiring room until it is an acceptable hour. No one of any import arrives before the second act. Now, inside quickly, both of you. I cannot be seen yet."

Anna's quiet chuckle warmed my chest as Lady Rycliffe ushered us inside.

Fifteen

THEATRE ROYALE, DRURY LANE, LONDON -
MARCH 5, 1814

I HAD BEEN to the theater as a guest a few times in the past, but I tried to experience it through new eyes, Anna's eyes. Her delight was palpable. Even Lady Rycliffe, in her haste not to be observed, was willing to slow her pace to allow Anna to look her fill. Her enthusiasm was infectious.

Eventually, though, Lady Rycliffe would not be delayed further and ushered us to her box. The seats were clearly purchased to see and be seen in, rather than to enjoy the show. Still, the view of the stage was good, and we would certainly be able to hear performers over the dull roar of the crowd.

Once Anna was settled into the best seat for actual viewing, I took the spot next to her while Lady Rycliffe took her place much farther back, away from the prying eyes of the *ton* but not so far as to neglect her chaperone duties.

"It's even more wonderful than I imagined." Anna's voice was barely a whisper, but her awe was delectable. She turned her grin on me. I could do little more than return it. She was entranced by the rich fabrics and twinkling chandeliers, the detail on the ceiling above us, the ornate set pieces, everything. Lady Rycliffe's box was one of the first to receive gas lamps, which were dimmed for the performance. Shrouding Anna and me in the privacy of darkness.

From Anna's reactions, I assumed the performance was acceptable. I was primarily engaged in watching her. The first act passed quickly amid a flurry of gasps and giggles from the woman beside me. Lady Rycliffe, now tardy enough for the masses, slipped through the curtains to visit with friends. Anna and I were left to our own devices.

Anna leaned over and whispered, "Augie, this is incredible."

I had no idea if that was the case, but I was more than happy to take her word for it. "I'm glad you're pleased."

She was so damn beautiful in the flickering chandelier light. Her curls danced in the glow from the flames, and her skin gleamed like pearls. Her eyes twinkled with delight. And the fine silk of her gown—I'd never seen her in anything so delicate. It suited her. Not that her usual dresses didn't flatter, but this... this was more bare skin than I had been blessed with since her hems had been lowered. Smooth, pale skin with a dusting of freckles. How far down did they go, I wondered.

My blatant ogling was interrupted by the sight of her gloved hand. It rested palm up, open on her knee. Expectant. Hopeful. Waiting for mine.

Plucking up more courage than I knew I was capable of, I brushed the littlest finger of my gloved hand against her wrist. She didn't pull away.

With a fortifying breath, I forged on. Sliding my hand up, I laced my fingers between hers. Slowly, gently, she tightened her grip. My heart twirled in delighted ecstasy at the sight.

Cursing the fabric of our gloves, and not for the first time, I felt only the heat of her, none of the sweet softness I was certain lay beneath our respective leather and silk prisons.

Glancing up, I saw her delicate lashes brush her cheek where she was staring at our joined hands. Her lips were parted enticingly, and I wanted desperately to take them in my own.

Abruptly, she broke our hands apart, and my heart lurched in terror. Before I could issue an apology, beg desperately for forgiveness, she surprised me once again.

Bringing her long elegant fingers to meet her other hand, she caught the tip of her glove between the opposite thumb and forefinger and tugged. She repeated the motion with each of her fingers and thumb. Suitably loosened, the glove slipped off with a final tug.

Long lines of alabaster skin dotted with constellations of freckles revealed themselves to me.

She dropped the first glove into her lap with a sidelong glance at me before working the second free.

Then, without comment, she settled her hand back where it had been between us. I moved to place mine back in hers, but she caught my wrist with her other hand, the prostrate one coming up to join.

She waited until my confused eyes met her certain ones, then tugged on the tip of the glove on my middle finger, followed by the first, third, and littlest. When she loosened the thumb, I finally understood.

Breathing shallow, I darted my tongue out to wet my lips. When she gave another, more decisive tug on the glove, I gasped.

It was, perhaps, the single most erotic moment of my life. The bare skin of my hand brushed against hers, our fingers slotting together as if they were made to fit. Two halves now whole.

Even more astonishing, she tightened her hold, dragging my hand to rest in her lap. Once situated, she moved her other hand, which landed atop mine.

She abandoned any attention once devoted to the goings on onstage. Instead, she inspected the lines and dips of my hand, running her graceful fingertips along my own, sending shivers down my spine with the gentle touch.

She could keep my hand forever if that was what she intended to do with it. Hell, she could keep it if she wanted to do anything else with it as well.

After a moment, she shifted, leaning closer. "Augie, would you consider walking me back to the house? I was hoping to find a few private moments."

Even I knew it was too early to make such an offer just yet, but I would walk with her anywhere. "I would be honored."

I pulled Anna's hand to me, taking my own opportunity to trace her long, delicate fingers with well-groomed nails. I always admired their graceful dexterity.

In youth, the nail beds were constantly caked with flour or dough. She kept her nails shorter when we were young too. Now they were longer, elegant.

A tiny, long-healed burn scar sat on the side of her thumb. I remembered the incident. I'd tried desperately to make her laugh between her tears while her mother cleaned and dressed the wound. It was formed in the pursuit of the perfect sourdough.

A second scar called the side of her ring-finger home. I didn't know its origin, and that bothered me more than I cared to admit. I wanted to know the story behind every single scar.

The back of her hand bore swirls and patterns of freckles. Her palm, though, held just one. It resided at the base of her forefinger, small and dark and shaped like a heart. Without permission, I pulled her palm to my lips, kissing it.

Her quiet gasp brought me back to myself, but she didn't wrest her hand from mine.

The curtain behind us fluttered open, and Lady Rycliffe dipped back inside.

Anna turned to address her in a whisper but made no

move to remove her hand from mine. "Lady Rycliffe, I was—we were hoping that Augie might walk me home. If you don't mind terribly?"

"Well, seeing what you two get up to when left alone, I see no harm in it." Lady Rycliffe commented with a nod toward our hands. Anna made a move to free her hand, but I held tight.

The audience around us began their applause. It was my first indication that significant time had passed. Anna wore her startled expression delicately. I wasn't the only unobservant one.

"Go, before the crush," Lady Rycliffe directed.

We slipped out from the box. I wavered between guilt at distracting Anna from the play and delight at my success. After all, I was always distracted by her, so it was only fair.

We escaped before the worst of the masses and slipped away. Once we passed the carriages, the streets quickly quieted. It was not so late as to be dangerous. Fortunately, it was an unseasonably warm night, and we ambled slowly down the lane. She was tucked tightly against my side, brushing against me every few steps.

"Thank you, for tonight, Augie. It was wonderful." Her earnest smile left me confident for my advance.

"It was. I hope we can do it again, or something similar. I believe there's a concert next Thursday."

Her face fell slightly, and she turned away from me, pulling apart from my side. She continued walking, a bit more briskly.

"I do not think Kate can spare me." My stomach flipped in distress.

"With all due respect, she didn't seem concerned tonight."

"Yes, but this was just one night. If it were to become a regular—" Her voice was quiet, tight. Almost as if she were holding back tears.

I paused our journey under a streetlamp and turned her to face me. We were still physically close but with a distance between us. I didn't care for it, but it seemed necessary for her.

"Anna, is this really about your work?" Her mouth opened and closed several times, about to start before she thought better of it. "Is there"—I swallowed the thought I needed to voice—"is there someone else?"

"No, there has never been anyone but you." *Oh, oh yes!*

"Then what is the problem?"

"There has never been anyone but you! But you left. You left me, and you kept abandoning me again and again and again. I know Michael needed your assistance, but not for eleven years! You could have come back to me at any time, but you didn't." Her eyes, near olive in the deep light, welled with tears. "How can I trust you not to leave again?"

I recoiled as if slapped. I wish she had. It would have hurt less. My heart cracked in two, anguish pouring forth from inside, spreading through me, burning all the while.

My first thoughts were to impress upon her that it had all been for her, that I was building a future for us. But the dream that had pushed me forward for more than a decade, moved me further, worked me harder, suddenly seemed so immaterial.

She had never asked for a provider. Hadn't she told me once, all those years ago? She'd said her dreams were smaller then. I had insisted that the right man would support her bigger dreams. Doggedly, I set about becoming the man of those bigger dreams. The man *I* decided she wanted. If the sinking feeling burrowing into my stomach was any indication, that man was far from what she had needed all along.

I swallowed back the lump that had made my throat its home and pulled her closer, pressing my forehead against her own. Her sweet scent enveloped me, still a hint of pastry even with no indication that she'd touched dough in months.

"You're right. I've been a dolt. I decided it was more important to become a man who could provide the means to make all your dreams come true. I failed to listen when you told me what those dreams were."

"Augie..."

"But, Anna, I've loved you since the first moment I saw you. I've loved you more every day since. And I'm listening now. I will do whatever it takes for you to trust me again. To prove to you that I am the one for you. There will never be anyone else for me. Please, tell me it's not too late."

I couldn't have stopped myself from cupping her jaw if my life depended on it. Her hand found its way onto my forearm. At first, I thought she meant to push me away, but she just grasped me, keeping me in place. As if I could go elsewhere.

"Perhaps we should continue with the weekly dinners? Just for now? Get to know each other better as adults?"

It was the opposite of what I wished for, more distance, more time spent in company with little in the way of private conversation. But I had promised whatever it took and I meant it.

"Yes, of course." I pressed a delicate kiss to her cheek before pulling back once more, tucking her arm in the crook of mine. Continuing along the sidewalk back toward Grayson House.

"I'm sorry," she whispered.

"Don't apologize. Not for this. If you wouldn't mind doing me a favor though?" We were mere steps away from the entry now, minutes from night's end.

"Anything."

"If you think of anything else I can do, you will let me know?" She nodded solemnly. "And perhaps keep the dress if you're able? It's as though it was made for you."

"Oh, it was. Or rather, re-made. There wasn't time for anything from the modiste, but Kate's friend, Juliet, is quite skilled with sewing. It's a gown she felt didn't suit her, so she said I could keep it." She stepped back and twirled the silky skirts around her, looking admiringly at her gown.

"Lovely." And she was the picture of loveliness. "I shall see you Wednesday?" She nodded quietly. "Good night, Anna."

"Good night, Augie."

Sixteen

WAYLAND'S, LONDON - MARCH 9, 1814

THE DAYS between the theater and our weekly dinner were agonizing. Michael was unbearably preoccupied. Apparently, he was still fretting over the fact that he'd made a right arse of himself in front of Westfield's daughter. The girl was reportedly quite fetching.

He and Lady Rycliffe seemed to have ended their liaison as well—the morning of our theater outing. Frankly it was a wonder she let us use her box and attended. The woman was a saint and not simply for putting up with him for two years.

The man vacillated between determination to stay away from Lady Juliet, and scheming ways to spend time with her. He practically wrote poetry to the prim, gentle, very affianced young lady. I'd listened to more debate over whether she was likely to be at supper this evening than I cared to recall. I was of the opinion that it was unlikely given past evidence—she had never been before.

More than once, I had been tempted to fabricate a reason for him to visit Johnson once more. His punch would certainly be more efficacious than mine. Perhaps, if the man hit his mouth this time, the incessant talking would cease.

I achieved little in the way of actual work, though slightly more than Michael. At least I kept my raptures to myself. Or I had after I gave Michael a summary of the events of Saturday night.

Every once in a while, he threw out an "I told you..." in regard to Anna's feelings for me. It was unnecessary at best. As if I could forget her telling me that she'd cared for me as long as I had her. Of course, the elation from that thought was immediately dimmed by the caveat that had followed.

I made the decision to choose optimism in the face of such an obstacle. Either way, it was no hardship to woo her.

While I'd promised to move at her pace, I hadn't promised to forgo flowers. I found I quite liked selecting them for her, choosing the ones that reminded me of her. I had the florist wrap the entire bouquet in lace tied with a sage ribbon that seemed similar to her new gown. I hoped the effect was not too far outside the spirit of our agreement that night.

Michael had no shortage of commentary on the flowers, but I paid him no mind. He was desperately trying to find a way to sneak the mysterious Lady Juliet a book. At least my quarry was not yet betrothed to another man. And wasn't that a sickening thought?

After knocking on the servants' entrance, I was greeted by the entrancing sight of my Anna on the other side of the threshold. She was back in her maid's uniform looking every bit as pretty as she had fancied up in her gown on Saturday. She took the procured flowers with no complaint and went so far as to press a kiss to my cheek in thanks.

I made every effort to remain the perfect gentleman. The loud, jovial dinner in the servants' quarters was spent brushing my elbow against Anna's side as subtly as I could manage. It ended with another kiss to my cheek and a soft, "I'll see you next week."

"You will." It was a vow I offered her. Nothing could keep me from this door at seven on Wednesday night.

"Unless, I don't suppose you would be willing to give me a tour of the club?" I hadn't expected that question, nor was I entirely comfortable with the idea of her in the gaming hell filled with degenerates and drunkards. Still, I was hardly going to turn down the opportunity to see her.

"I await your convenience. Name a time."

"Sunday? After church?"

She could not have selected a more appropriate time. I was unbearably grateful I wouldn't have to toss out the reprobates before she arrived. One sight of her and half the members would be barred for comments and behavior I found objectionable. The club was always nearly empty on Sundays just after church, though. The few hours when our members chose to play at being family men.

"I look forward to it."

IF I SPENT the entirety of the days that followed frantically sorting out the disastrous state of my office, I would never admit it. I would need to discuss a promotion for Baldwin with Michael. The man was performing far outside of his duties while the two of us fluttered about like lovesick milksops. Long-married, Baldwin seemed to find the entire situation amusing, so there was at least that consolation for his increased duties.

When the day finally arrived, I walked to Grayson House. I left far earlier than appropriate. The sun was high, but the day was brisk, and I was beginning to fret over my choice to leave the carriage behind. Ladies' frocks were so thin and delicate, and their pelisses offered little in the way of warmth.

Just as I was about to climb the steps, Anna stepped out, closing the door behind her.

"I was going to…"

"I know, but I wished to spare you the curious stares this time," she said with a deprecating grin.

"Still?"

"There was quite an interrogation at breakfast the morning after we went to the theater. Several of the footmen and Stevens were hoping to earn an invitation today as well."

I hesitated for only a moment. "They are welcome to join us if you would like."

"I would not. And not one of them has the coin to lose."

"Very well. I hadn't anticipated the chill today. Shall I hire a hack?"

"Not at all. Kate's friend and I are very much the same size. She was happy to lend me a pelisse. I am beginning to suspect they enjoy dressing me like a doll."

Distracted as I had been with her comfort, I hadn't taken a moment to appreciate her efforts today. Her dress was a simple, unadorned, blue-green like a robin's egg, and the pelisse was a darker shade of the same. She also wore a straw bonnet with matching ribbon. I couldn't recall ever seeing her wear one and, though it framed her face enticingly, I cursed the covering of her hair.

"A very fetching doll." I was rewarded with a smile before she tucked her arm in mine and we set off. She did not seem to feel the chill overly but when the wind offered a particularly strong gust, she pressed in closer to me. Overall, my decision to skip the carriage had been a good one.

My nerves grew the closer we came to the club. I wished her to be impressed, of course, but also, my work as bookmaker had taken me away from her. It was the point of contention in our budding relationship.

I would leave, if it meant she would be my wife, but I did

enjoy my work. I had fallen into the role by circumstance more than I had chosen it, but I was quite skilled at my job, and I had hoped for many more years there.

Anna, perhaps sensing my unease, chattered gayly about the weather. I was paying unforgivably little attention when she tugged my sleeve gently. "I'm sorry, I—"

"Augie, relax. I am excited to see what you've built."

I nodded breathlessly.

"I apologize for my inattention, regardless."

"Did you think I never felt nerves presenting you with a new recipe?"

"You did?"

"Apparently, you did," she muttered. "Yes, quite nervous. Your opinion is the one that matters most to me."

"Anna..."

"I believe we've arrived, at least if the name on the door is any indication."

"Ah, yes." I made a valiant effort to shake off my nerves and pulled the heavy wooden door open for her. "Welcome to Wayland's."

Before she took her first step inside the open, round room, her jaw slipped open slightly. Just a few steps inside, she paused, spinning around slowly. She took in the high domed ceiling and dramatic red curtains lining the enormous support pillars, the plush emerald gaming tables, extensive cherry bar with hundreds of bottles stair-stepped against the mirrored wall behind it, the ornate carpeting topping the floor.

Her spin stopped, and she observed the lavishly carved doors of the private rooms and the grand staircase wrapping around the wall to the rounded second floor, open to the view below by a hand-carved cherry banister. The same impressive doors were mirrored there, leading to our offices and file rooms.

"Augie..." Her tone gave none of her thoughts away. I

gestured for her hat and handed it to Potter as he passed. With any luck, he'd lose it and I would get to bask in the sight of her curls the entire walk home.

Personally, I thought Michael's taste bordered on ostentatious but the *ton* seemed generally impressed upon first viewing.

Her voice seemed to draw Michael's attention away from the game of hazard he was winning against Baron James. The only thing smaller than the man's skill level was his pocketbook at this point. He continued to wager far beyond his means. He'd married a pretty, well-admired wife a few months ago, and the resulting influx of cash was steadily making its way into Michael's pockets.

"Anna! I intended to accompany Augie and lost track of the time." He'd intended to accompany me and, by strange coincidence, I left when he was otherwise occupied—how remiss of me. "Welcome! Can we get you something to drink? Or would you like a tour, perhaps? Augie has been frantically cleaning the place in hopes of impressing you."

She glanced down at the pile of Michael's winnings and blanched while I glared at the man. It wasn't a particularly large sum for Michael, especially after playing all night. But it was enough to bankrupt a light-in-the-pocket noble like James. They must have had other players who had abandoned the table. Michael generally made it a point not to personally ruin anyone. What the gentlemen did among themselves in his club was not his concern.

"Michael... that's—" She nodded toward his winnings.

"Oh, yes. Slow night." The baron *harrumphed*. "Can we have someone fetch you some tea?"

"Slow... I think I may need something stronger than tea."

Anna didn't drink often as a rule, so the request was somewhat surprising. I urged her gently over to a seat at the bar. It was becoming apparent that, at some point, I had grown accustomed to the excesses of the beau monde. Michael's winnings were quite light, really. I suspected he was going easy on his opponent.

I slipped behind the bar and turned toward her to see what she might like, but Anna's face remained frozen in something akin to shock. Instead, I grabbed a brandy I thought she might favor and poured a glass, then pressed it gently into her hand. She swallowed it without seeming to taste it. I hesitated before pouring another, watering it down slightly. She sipped this one, still taking in the opulence around her.

Drink in hand, she turned to me. "Is there... do you have an office?"

"Yes. Would you like to see it?" She nodded and stood. I pressed her free hand into my elbow, leading her up the curved staircase to the second door we came across on the top floor. Once inside, I intended to leave the door open after she followed me in. Instead, she pressed back against it, pushing it closed behind her.

Seventeen

THE NOISE OF THE CLUB, light as it was so early on a Sunday, disappeared with the click of the door. For such a tiny sound, it was powerful.

Anna stared at me, pressed against the door with wide eyes for a long moment. "Augie, I had no idea."

"I... I don't understand. What's wrong?"

"Augie, I knew you were successful, but this... no wonder you never... Michael is casually playing for a life-changing sum as we speak. I would never need to work again. My children would never need to work. Their children as well. And it's a 'slow' night?" Her breaths came in sharp pants, and I was making a concerted effort to focus on her words rather than the enticing effect it was having on her bosom.

"Anna, I don't—"

"And you just... you let me complain that you never visited... What are you even doing with me? For sums such as that you could have any lady you wanted."

It took nearly a full minute for me to comprehend what she was saying. She actually thought...

"All right, this is not the important point, but I want to

put this idea to rest first. That sum down there goes into Michael's personal funds. He doesn't gamble with club money. Not since he earned enough to fund it. Second, I don't gamble at all any more. I'm paid a salary. It's more substantial than I deserve for the work I do, but I'm not seeing sums like that on a nightly basis."

I took a step back toward her, pressing in close. Caging her to the door. I tipped her chin up with two fingers and couldn't resist brushing my thumb across her lower lip as her gaze met mine, then I slid my hand to cup her cheek.

"Third, and most importantly, Anna Hudson, there is not a single woman in the entire world I want more than you. I know you know that. I may have been a pathetic coward, but I haven't been subtle, and you're whip smart."

"Why?" her voice cracked on the question, and she darted her tongue out to wet her lower lip. The sight induced a groan no dam could have held back. I let my forehead fall to the door beside her with a *thunk*. Her enticing scent enveloped me once again.

My answer was brushed, hot, against her ear. "You need me to list all the reasons I want you?" I felt her answering nod, curls brushing my cheek. I shocked her by pulling away, a gasp escaping, before I caught her hand in my own and slid my other one low along her waist. I directed her toward the oversized gilded mirror that overtook the wall opposite the fireplace. I guided her in front of me, centering her in the glass, before pressing myself in behind her, resting my chin on her shoulder. The long, lean lines of her back pressed against my front in all sorts of delicious ways.

"Look at you," I whispered low in her ear and was rewarded with a shudder. "How could I want anyone else? I can't help but think of you every time I see the sunset. That's what I thought—the first time we met—this hair." I paused and pulled back just slightly to release one pin from her thick curls, then a second, a third, until they fell around her shoulders in silken waves. A sea on fire.

"The gold, and copper on top, but underneath auburn and mahogany." For the first time, I ran a single finger along a thick red ringlet. I didn't trust myself further than that, but even the limited touch was incredible.

"And your eyes. They change with your mood and the light. Sometimes, like now, they're more gray than green, like the sky before a storm. Sometimes they're more of a forest color. When you're happy, the gold in the center is more noticeable, and they're olive."

I paused to run a hand along the side of her neck. "And these freckles. I've dreamed of tasting them since I was old enough to understand desire."

"Augie..."

"And Anna, how could I possibly think of anyone else when every time I so much as look at a pastry, I can't help but think of you? How yours would be better, always, every time. And you still smell like home, spices and flour, kitchen fires, and fresh air."

"I haven't touched flour in months, Augie."

"I know. It doesn't matter. And stop interrupting. You're distracting me. Look how well we fit together." I pulled her back against me, tighter, leaving my hand low on her hip. Allowing her to feel what she did to me. She gave me a breathless smile in return. "And your smile... your entire face brightens when you smile. But all that—it's just the physical. I love your heart most of all. You care so much for everyone around you. You cared for my father during his darkest days, as though he were your own. I will never be able to repay you for that kindness."

I brushed my lips against her temple before continuing. "And this mind... You're so far ahead of everyone else. You run circles around the rest of us. The way you're not afraid to tease me... I adore it. Makes my heart flip every time. How could I not love you, Anna? How could there be anyone else in the world for me after I met you? You're incredible."

She turned in the circle of my arms to face me. "Augie..." She shook her head. Then she surprised me by sliding the hand grasping my arm to the back of my neck, pulling me down the inch or so between us to her lips.

For the briefest second, it was awkward until we both tilted slightly, found the angle, and slotted together just so. The ground dropped out from under me. I was falling, and it was *exhilarating*. My hand found her jaw, and her fingers speared through my hair, tugging me impossibly closer. The hand on her waist flexed tighter with a mind of its own, feeling the elegant line of her side through far too many layers. Her answer was a soft, sensuous whimper against my mouth.

Gathering all my self-control and some I wasn't aware I possessed, I pulled away from her. When her lips chased mine, I almost broke but managed to remain strong.

"Anna." It was all I managed between panting breaths. "Anna, we need to stop."

Her answer was a whine I'd never heard from her before. "Why?"

"I was earning your trust, remember. Proving that I can be here for you?"

"Why are you so coherent right now? I can't remember anything but your name." My forehead fell to her shoulder as I groaned at the images her words conjured.

"You will be disappointed in me if I allow this to go further before we're ready." It served as a reminder to myself but also seemed to cool her ardor slightly.

She pulled farther away, wiping her palms on her dress. "I'm sorry. I didn't intend to attack you."

"If that is your manner of attack, I hope you feel free to do so again at your leisure." That earned me a giggle, and she seemed to relax.

I directed her toward one of the wingback chairs by the fire and pulled out the file I'd organized in preparation for her visit before I joined her. "I want you to know, I understood you when you told me the bakery wasn't your dream anymore. But in case you still wanted to explore that option, I've been researching this for quite some time. I thought you should have it."

"What is it?"

"Locations, projected costs and earnings, necessary documents for a bakery. If you decide this is something you want, I want to help you. Even if it's not as your husband. I could give you the funds." She began to protest here, but I soldiered on. "Or it could be a loan if you prefer. I'm certain Michael would invest if you would feel more comfortable working with him. If you would rather cast this to the fire, I would be happy to do so. I just wanted you to have the choice."

She flipped through the documents, pulling the occasional page from the file to observe closer. "You... you researched the best locations for a bakery?" I nodded in response, unease growing inside the longer her reaction remained subdued. "And the costs and potential earnings?"

"Yes."

She looked up at me then. "How long?"

"Ten years or so? Around the time it seemed Michael would win enough to actually pay us all. The older plans are a bit more sparing. I had assumed we'd have less to start. But I promise, if you choose me, I will die a happy man. If you wish to remain a lady's maid, well, I may have to purchase an estate next to Thornton Hall so I can actually see you, but I will be very happy for you. If you do not wish to work at all, I can support us quite comfortably. But if you wish to open a bakery, we can make that happen for you." I fought back against the urge to keep talking, throwing forth desperate options until she agreed to one—agreed to be mine.

"Show me?" Immediately, I dragged my chair closer to her, allowing me to point out various aspects of properties as she flipped through them. Offering her the use of the club solicitor or a recommendation for one of her own if she preferred.

That was how Michael found us, hours later. Pressed together in front of the fire, piles sorted on the table before us. Anna's hair unbound, tousled from my hands, and glorious in the firelight.

Eighteen

ANNA HAD BEEN in the country for nearly three months. It was enough to drive a man to insanity. How was one expected to live on the memory of a single kiss? Just one taste of her lips.

Live on it I did, though, day and night. I thought of little else. It was a miracle the club hadn't burned to the ground in my distraction.

Michael had gone off with them in a pathetic attempt both to woo and simultaneously not woo the still-engaged Lady Juliet. I did pity the besotted man. At least Anna, though miles away, had the potential to be mine. I had been using my regular correspondence with Michael to send and receive letters from Anna.

The dangerous game he was playing with Lady Juliet had come to a head a fortnight ago, and he had returned briefly only to disappear with a large sum of money and an even larger bottle of whiskey. I hadn't been able to locate him, though I expected he did not particularly wish to be found. His return put an end to any communication with Anna that wouldn't compromise her beyond belief. Much as the thought

ALLY HUDSON

of forcing a wedding was tempting, I would not take the choice from her.

But she had arrived home last evening, and I could not be convinced to wait even a moment longer. It was far too early for callers, but that didn't stop me from knocking on the servants' entrance, dahlias in hand. Weston greeted me politely and nodded toward the kitchens. There, in the center of the long oak table, was a plate of raspberry tarts with a note beside them with nothing more than my name, underlined thrice in Anna's elegant script.

I froze in the middle of the room, staring stupidly at the tarts. I knew it was illogical. She could have made them simply because she felt the urge, but somehow, I was certain it meant more. Tears welled unbidden in my eyes. On numb legs, I made my way to the tarts and settled before them.

They were perfect. She had never made a more perfect tart; I was positive of it. I couldn't bring myself to eat one for a long moment, but when I finally took a bite, they were the single best things I had ever eaten. It was senseless. The berries were sweet and tart. They should have been just barely in season, but they were ripened to perfection. The pastry was buttery and flakey and tender and incredible.

That was how she found me, staring awe-struck at a plate of tarts. She sat across from me and pulled a folded page out of her apron. On it was one of the locations from the file. I examined it; the location was just down the street from the club. Across from my apartments. There were locations across the city in that file. Hell, there were locations in Kent. But she'd chosen that one.

"Anna..."

"A loan, I think. I want to prove I can do it on my own."

"Of course," my answer was hoarse around the tightness in my throat.

"The loan and a courtship. I'd like to be wooed properly, I think. I suspect you're rather good at it."

"I've never tried, but I'm feeling quite inspired." I nodded toward the flowers I'd forgotten at the sight of the tarts.

She inhaled their scent delicately, smiling softly. "I'm afraid I've grown accustomed to flowers, sir. Developing plans to bring my childhood dreams to life as well... it's quite the overdone thing, you see."

"Is it? Do you have a suggestion then? Perhaps I should purchase a castle? I hear there are a great many in Scotland." She shook her head indulgently.

"Alas, I expect creativity out of my suitors. I can't possibly offer suggestions."

"Very well, I am left to my own intuition. Are you available for a promenade? Or has your return from the countryside left you with mountains of work?"

"Quite the latter, unfortunately. Perhaps later this week?"

"I am available at your convenience. How did you find Kent?"

"It was lovely as always. Michael made quite a mess of it with Lady Juliet, though. Compromised her quite thoroughly, then up and left without a word. I don't suppose he's at the club? I've quite a few things to say to him."

"I fear, given the state I saw him in last, he's unlikely to survive a tongue lashing from you. I've been unable to locate him for weeks. I suspect he's held up somewhere losing outrageous sums of money. She is ruined? That is unlike him, to compromise an innocent."

"She may survive unscathed. After all, it was the country, not Town. But her heart has taken quite the beating."

"If your words don't end him, I might."

"Such teamwork. A promising future for us. I really must return to my duties now. I will see you soon?"

"I thought to set up a meeting with my solicitor at his

earliest convenience. Perhaps we may partake in a promenade after?"

"That sounds wonderful." Her lips brushed a delicate kiss to my cheek. It was less than I had hoped for, but more than I deserved. My heart skipped regardless. Then she shooed me out the door, tarts in hand.

OVER THE NEXT FEW DAYS, Tom joined in the search for Michael. Apparently, even Anna's depiction of Lady Juliet's distress was understated. I was now certain I couldn't possibly give him the thrashing he deserved, and I would have to turn him over to Johnson to use as a training post. The search for my missing employer continued while I managed the club with a great deal of assistance from Baldwin. I had given the man a raise in Michael's absence. It was not as though he was available to object.

In the interim, I managed to set up a meeting with the club's solicitor for Anna and myself in just under a fortnight's time on July 1. I also approached the owner of the bakery site for a figure at which they would be willing to sell. It was certainly too high, particularly for an unoccupied building. I was confident I could offer him a substantially lower sum and he would jump at the chance. Given Anna's desire for a loan, I needed to keep costs low.

I called at Grayson House every night, even if only for a few moments. She visited the club once again, and the temptation presented by my closed study door proved to be too much for us. She escaped the encounter slightly mussed.

The largest surprise came only a few days after Anna's return. Early in the day, Baldwin opened the club door to a gentle young woman with dark curls and unearthly blue eyes, far too innocent for one of the usual female guests. Lady

Juliet. She had been searching for Michael and was disappointed to find only me.

After seeing the sadness in her eyes myself, I determined that perhaps not even Johnson's fists would be sufficient. The fool man had won her heart and ran away from the responsibility of its safekeeping.

She told me she was determined to end her engagement to Rosehill, who was proving recalcitrant. He left her but one way out of the engagement, ruination. Fortunately, the club owned the majority of her father's debts. We would call them in, publicly. In doing so, she would be left ruined and Rosehill would have no choice but to release her. Leaving her free to wed Michael. If he hadn't managed to land himself in debtor's prison in the interim. He would owe me a raise if this all went to plan. Sorting out his romantic life was not in the position description.

She was staying with the viscountess at Grayson House, so meeting with her was no difficulty. Hugh and Agatha remained in the country. Anna expressed some worry about the state of that marriage as well, but I could only sort the romantic woes of one brother at a time. Particularly whilst wooing a particularly fetching baker.

And woo I did. I arrived with ever more elaborate floral arrangements. The occasional jewel also made an appearance. So, too, did the most intriguing spices to be had at the docks. Cooking wares were also a feature, the best I could find on offer. Those had netted me the most enthusiastic kiss in response. A kiss I spent many an evening and early morning considering at length. A kiss a man could live on with ease.

Nineteen

JULY DAWNED with the promise of a busy day. Richard Dalton—Lord Westfield—was to be arrested at Lady James's ball that evening. I spent all week purchasing his other outstanding debts and ensuring the arrest would happen dramatically on the ballroom floor. But first, Anna and I were to meet with the solicitor.

I had been sorting through some documents in Michael's office that I had neglected in recent days. Baldwin had done an excellent job managing the club. I was astounded when Michael himself appeared in the doorway. I hadn't seen him in weeks. He was certainly worse for wear, but recently bathed, at least. He told me he'd had some sense knocked into him, by Dalton of all people, and was determined to make Lady Juliet his own.

He was pleased with the plan we'd concocted in his absence and a nervous wreck over her acceptance of his suit. I left him to his flutterings and spasms in time to meet with Anna and the solicitor.

The day was fine and the woman at my side, wearing a blue-green day dress, was as fetching as always. She'd worn her hair pulled back simply. I assumed in an effort to appear professional. She'd scolded me when I tried to muss it with my hands whilst taking her lips with mine. After we had broken apart, of course. She was otherwise occupied during the mussing. She was nervous, though, and there was a flush to her cheeks that could not be owed to the weather or my attentions. After all, our solicitor was but a few blocks walk from Grayson House.

Will Hart was a kind man in his midthirties with a penchant for numbers and an eye for business. He had proven himself invaluable when Michael and I first began the club, and I had no doubt he would treat Anna's bakery with the respect it deserved. Not all solicitors would be willing to work with a woman, particularly an unmarried one. But I had no concerns from his quarter. All that besides, he could read between the lines, and the club was certainly an account he couldn't afford to lose.

He greeted Anna with alacrity, displayed all due enthusiasm for her plans, and laid out the options available to her. He treated her with the dignity he showed Michael and me, and the bakery with the importance of the club.

It was decided that I would purchase the property outright, and Anna would pay me back out of her profits when they began to come in. I would also provide a loan for the starting material costs, which would be repaid as well. Anna insisted on paying interest but with a glare from me. Will was smart enough to mention a rate well below market.

When we left, he was drawing up the purchase papers for the building. I had managed to get the owner down to a far more reasonable rate, and it was entirely feasible for Anna to run the bakery profitably.

Once we stepped out of the crowded office, Anna shook the nerves from her hands before lamenting that time didn't allow for a promenade. She had to ready Lady Juliet for the ball, and I needed to ensure everything was in place for Dalton —Westfield's—arrest.

I turned us in the direction of the house, her hand tucked once again in my arm. "That was incredible, Augie. Is it always like that?" She was nearly giddy with excitement.

"Not always. Eventually, it becomes routine. But the first few meetings, yes. At least with Will. Michael and I met with a few shiftier solicitors before finding him. Just wait until you're handed the key to the bakery."

"I'm grateful for your help. I don't know how I would find someone reputable on my own."

"I thought he would treat you well. You're pleased with the results of the meeting then?"

"I'm delighted. The day is nearly perfect."

"Nearly?"

"Yes, nearly." Her reply was prim and her smile knowing and mysterious.

"Do you have any suggestions for achieving perfection?"

"Come to the house after the business with Juliet's father is finished?"

"It may be quite late."

"I don't mind. Please?" We were at the door now, her back pressed against it.

"Anything for you."

She pressed a kiss to my lips that was over far too quickly before she slipped inside. Half closing the door, she whispered, "I'll see you tonight."

I was left to nod mutely at the closed door.

THE FIRST PART of Juliet's plan went smoothly. Her father was dragged from the ballroom and carted off to debtor's prison with much fanfare.

Knowing Michael was waiting for her inside, I felt more confident allowing her entry to Lady James's ball. I was not certain he had received an actual invitation, but I imagined he would waive some of the baron's debts in exchange for entry if questioned.

I had assumed my nervous feelings would dissipate after the arrest, but they seemed only to grow as I made my way through the darkened streets of London. I was unwilling to wait for a hack, and I wanted to ensure the carriage was there for Juliet if she needed it.

The walk to Grayson House was short, but the minutes dragged. There was something in the air, anticipation thrummed.

I had barely finished knocking on the back entry when Anna opened the door. Instead of the usual flurry of servants, it was just her. She was in her maid uniform but her hair was loose and unbound, free for my exploration. The entire kitchen smelled of some unfamiliar spice and the comforting scent of Anna's pastries.

"Where is everyone?"

"Juliet gave us the evening off since it's just her tonight. I offered to wait until she returned to let her in."

"The viscountess?"

"Gone to Lincolnshire to assist her sister through confinement."

"Hugh? Agatha?"

"Kent. Anyone else you wish to inquire about?"

"We're alone?"

"Everyone else is down at the tavern."

She'd hardly finished the sentence before I tangled a hand in the hair at the back of her neck and pulled her lips to mine. Far from complaining, she made an effort to direct me toward the center of the room, then pushed me down on the bench seat with the table to my back.

My mouth fell from hers with a groan, following her directions. She proceeded to shock every thought from my mind by resting a knee on the bench to the outside of my thigh, then the second, straddling my lap. Her lips were kiss swollen, and she had never been more beautiful.

"Anna..." I moved to take back her lips, but she pressed a delicate finger against mine, keeping me in place.

She gave a nervous swallow before starting. "Augie... Do you wish to get married? To me?"

She was... But I should—I shook away the muddled thoughts. "Yes! More than anything."

Her smile was blinding, and I reached up once more, desperate to seal our agreement with a kiss, only for her firm hand on my chest to stop me in my place.

"I'm an unconventional woman, Augie, but not that unconventional. You may propose to me properly." My heart stopped for a moment, before pounding with more force than ever before.

"Now?"

"If you please."

If I'd been given half a moment to overthink this, I would have stumbled over the words. As it was, they came unbidden, perfect in their instinct.

"Anna Hudson, I thought I loved you the first day I met you. And I did, in all the ways a four-year-old knows how to love. But if I had known then what it was to love you now, I wouldn't have termed such a pale imitation *love*. Not a day has gone by over the last twenty-four years that I haven't thought of you, admired you, been inspired by your heart and your courage and your humor.

"If you do me the great honor of agreeing to be my wife, I will spend the rest of my days doing everything in my power to make each and every one of your dreams come true. You have been by my side on all of my very best days and held my hand through my very worst. I want to spend the rest of my life doing the same for you. Please, will you marry me?" My throat had gone thick with emotion halfway through, and tears had come to her eyes. I brushed them off her cheeks one by one.

She grabbed my neck with both hands tugging me in for a kiss that was all emotion and no skill. She pulled back and whispered a throaty "Yes" before returning her lips where they belonged. Elation and love filled me, threatening to over-whelm me. This woman—with hair like sunset, who smelled of pastry—had agreed to spend the rest of her life with me.

My determination to taste every available inch of neck and shoulder I managed to uncover was interrupted by a knock at the back door. My fiancée, far too disheveled for company, scrambled off my lap, tugging her dress back into place and gesturing at me to answer.

There was no small amount of grumbling required to perform that task, but I managed to open the door to find Michael and Juliet, both slightly more rumpled than they'd been when I last saw them earlier that evening.

"Looks like the ball went well then?"

"You could say that. Why are you here? Shouldn't you be watching my club?" Michael was far too smug for all the trouble he'd caused me these last weeks and months.

I led them into the kitchen, blocking Anna from view. Michael had no business seeing her in her fetching state of disarray.

"I've been watching your damn club for nearly three months. It's my night off."

"Since when do you have a night off?"

"Since I'm at least partially responsible for the foolish smile on your face. Now that you've returned, Anna and I will be leaving for the evening." She had righted her dress, but the lovely flush I'd caused remained, as well as the beginnings of a bruise on her neck. I must remember to be more careful with her delicate skin—no matter what delectable noises she made.

"Unless you need assistance, my lady?" I struggled to hold back a groan at her words. Of course, Anna would offer to help her. She was too kind for her own good. And mine.

Juliet declined, and Anna formed the beginnings of a protest. With little thought, I slid my arm behind my fiancée, covering her mouth with my hand. She put up a wriggle as a token protest and certain parts of my anatomy appreciated the gesture.

"We'll be going then. Enjoy your evening. I'll see you at the club tomorrow, Michael."

I had us half out the door before I finished the sentence. I didn't want to give either of them the opportunity for further interruptions.

In the alley, Anna dug her feet in, ceasing my tugging. "Cardamom Buns!"

"What?"

"I made you Cardamom Buns! With the spices you brought. I left them on the counter." She turned to go back to the house.

I tightened my grip on her hand in response. "Anna, my love, I mean this in the nicest possible way. I could not possibly care less about the buns. I want to taste *you*, not the pastry."

"Oh." Her eyes were wide as she processed my meaning.

"I promise to try them when I drop you off... in the morning."

"All right, but they won't be as good then." She allowed me to direct her out of the alley.

"I promise I will love them all the more for not delaying us tonight."

Her answering laugh was everything.

Twenty

"WOULD YOU LIKE A CUP OF TEA?" I asked, abandoning Anna at the door without a look. Desperate for some occupation, I moved to the kitchen to put the kettle on, anything to keep me from behaving like the brute I desperately wished to be.

I surveyed my apartment, and everything appeared to be in order. Clean and tidy. I didn't spend much of my day here, so that wasn't a terrible surprise. But now Anna was in it. And I desperately wanted her to find it acceptable. At least for tonight.

"I don't want any tea, Augie." She was still pressed against the door where I'd left her. Rudely.

My nerves would ruin this before it even started if I didn't calm down. Swallowing them, I returned to her side.

"Water?"

"I didn't come here for a drink."

Her tone was thick, sensual in a way I had never heard. Finally, I met her eyes. They were darker than I had ever seen them. She considered me thoughtfully, even... lustfully.

"What did you come here for?"

115

"You," she said simply, as though it was not the single most important three-letter word in existence.

"Anna." The groan ripped out of me, and my forehead *clunked* onto the door next to her ear.

"You asked." I could hear the smile in her voice as I inventoried the delicate skin of her neck.

"What do you want with me? I'll give you anything."

"Anything?"

"Anything," I promised.

"Maids talk, Augie. I've heard things..."

"I mean it, anything," I whispered in her ear before tasting the freckle just below it—sugared raspberries. How did she taste better than she smelled? It should not be possible.

"But—"

I pulled back from her neck to find her gaze. "Anna, I've had twenty years to fantasize about you. If there's something you want to try, I guarantee I've thought about it. A lot."

"That is quite a lot to live up to," she said, worrying her lower lip.

"Don't worry, just to kiss you... It was more incredible than every single one of the fantasies. Now, tell me about yours."

"I..." she breathed between us, trailing off with her full lower lip caught between her teeth. I pulled the delicate flesh free from her bite with a thumb before catching her jaw with my hand. I dipped down to catch that lip between mine. Then I gently nipped it before laving it with my tongue. Her head fell back against the door with a *thunk*—must protect her head —and a sensual sigh.

"Tell me, Anna. I want to make all your dreams come true. Tell me..." My lips found her neck again, the spot where it met her shoulder, the one that made her shudder.

"Your mouth..." she groaned. I couldn't tell if she was

praising my efforts or asking for more of them. Either option was delightful.

"What about it?" I exhaled against her skin, drawing down toward the bodice of her gown, trailing with lips and tongue. "Do you want it here?" I asked, drawing a finger just under the simple hem of her neckline. "Or here?" My other hand wound down to her thigh, rucking up her skirts as I dragged it upward to her center. Even through the mounds of skirt, the heat there burned.

Her only answer was a desperate moan and a hand tightening in my hair.

"Anna? Where do you want my mouth?"

"Everywhere…"

"Everywhere?" I asked, a smile pressed into the crevice between her breasts.

"Augie…" she whined. "I mean everywhere." Only Anna could tease me while pleading for me to fulfill one of my deepest desires.

I pulled away from her chest for a moment. Just for a second to enjoy the sight of my fiancée, mussed, flushed, and drugged with lust—for me. Satisfied that she was precisely as aroused as she ought to be, I pressed her back into the door. I grabbed one thigh, hitching it over my hip before adding the other.

A squeak escaped her, and she clung to me as I carried her to the bedroom. There, I set her on the oversized bed, covered in Anna's-eyes-green bedding. Now that I had her here, I finally confirmed that my match had been perfection itself.

And then I dropped to my knees before her. Leaning forward, I found the buttons at the back of her gown. I quirked a questioning brow, and she reached back to assist me without a word. Together, we freed her from the confines, leaving her in only crisp stays and a white chemise.

Damn, she was beauty itself.

Before I could divest her of the stays, she caught my hand. "Your turn."

Thought had left my brain when the gown left her body, so it took me a moment to comprehend her meaning. Anna wanted me less dressed; I could be less dressed. I ripped off the coat, tossing it off to the side. The cravat flew away too. Then the waistcoat was still buttoned and my fingers tangled there. I yanked it off and heard a button or two ping across the floor. My eagerness earned a sweet laugh from Anna. Stripping my suspenders before I pulled my shirt over my head, I tossed it to wherever was far away from us. Where the rest of the things that we would never need again belonged.

"Augie..." There was something unreadable in her tone.

"What?"

"You didn't look like that the last time I saw you..."

I laughed. There was a self-conscious inclination to retrieve the shirt, but I was fairly certain she was looking at me with interest—not revulsion—so I pressed it down.

"I was five and ten the last time you saw me without a shirt."

"I remember... And you didn't look like that."

"Good or bad?"

"So good. I thought it was good then as well, but... So, so good." And now I would never feel self-conscious again.

"Even then?" I asked.

"Oh, yes. Do you remember the mistletoe that year? I didn't speak to Mary for a month after she kissed you."

"You wanted to kiss me?" I blurted.

"I've wanted to kiss you since I was old enough to want to kiss anyone." She said it slowly, as though she were putting pieces together while she spoke.

"You did? But I thought... Michael?"

"What about him?" she asked, brow furrowed.

"I thought you wanted to kiss Michael."

"Why would I want to kiss Michael?"

"You never... I am the world's biggest dolt," I said, dragging a hand through my hair.

"You thought...?"

"You were talking with the other maids. You said he was handsome!"

"He is handsome. What has that to do with anything?"

"But..."

"Hugh is handsome, and I mostly want to knock his head against something hard," she said, adding, "Is that why you never...?"

"Yes..."

"You *are* the world's biggest dolt." There was something affectionate in her tone while she insulted me. I couldn't particularly disagree.

A thousand, million moments, previously tainted with a false understanding of her attraction to Michael were now shiny and new.

Anna had wanted me. Always.

"I am. But you've already agreed to marry me. I'm afraid I cannot release you."

"I am unbearably cross with you right now, Augustus Ainsley." She tried, unsuccessfully, to bite back the smile as she said it. "And I believe we learned how to end an engagement tonight."

"If you think I would release you over something so small as anyone you know being carted off to the gaol, you're mad, Anna Hudson. You are mine. And you always have been."

"I have." She leaned forward once again, grabbing my cheeks and holding me in place. Her lips found mine, sliding in to fit just so.

I pulled away just for a second. Breathing into the space between us, I whispered, "I'll make it up to you." And I caught her lips again.

I expected to be nervous for this, the culmination of every fantasy I'd ever had. But when I loosened Anna's stays and helped her pull the chemise over her wild curls, the awe drowned everything else away. Every single romantic, filthy thought I'd had about this moment was inadequate. There were miles of pale skin dusted with constellations of freckles, and all of her was laid bare, just for me.

A curse escaped me before my mouth found a better occupation. Her lips, her throat, her chest, her arms, her breasts, her stomach, her legs, her center, all were free for me to claim. And claim I did. Someday I would name the constellations of the night sky that was her skin—when I had hours, days, weeks, months, years to do so. It was too new, and she was too sweet to waste this time with words.

Delicate pants escaped her as I worshiped her, *everywhere* as requested. Every perfect inch of her tasted as good, better even, than her best tarts. When her long fingers found my hair, instructing me wordlessly, I was grateful. After all, I had work to do here. While she had assured me that she had no interest in Michael, past or present, I had to be certain she would never have an interest in anyone else, ever. Pleasuring her until she was a boneless, sated heap tangled in the bed coverings seemed as good a plan as any. Better than most of my others, really.

I managed to coax two climaxes out of her before she yanked my mouth away from the sweet haven between her thighs. My knees gave a token protest as she pulled me up the bed overtop her. Knees were pointless. I hadn't yet figured out how to please her with my knees so I hardly had need of them.

Her breath hitched when my trouser-clad hardness brushed against her overwrought core. My whimpered groan was less elegant.

"Sorry—sorry. I... We don't have to... I didn't mean..." Clearly my erection had overtaken my capacity for speech, and it wasn't inserted in chivalry or gentlemanly promises.

"I did," she breathed, before catching my lips with her own. Her tongue found mine with a downright filthy swipe. She found the fastenings of my trousers with the hand that wasn't still tangled in my hair. That one, trapped in the strands, gave a tug when I nipped at her lower lip. The yank was just shy of painful, and thoroughly arousing. Managing the lacings one handed was an impressive feat of hers. Even more impressive was when she used her legs and feet to shove my trousers down to the floor below. Never breaking away once.

I, however, required air. Pulling away, I whispered in the inch between us. "Anna..."

"Stop trying to talk me out of this. I want this—you."

Biting back another curse, I pulled away enough to run a hand over her core. My Anna, still ready, waiting for me.

In one breath, we were two. In the next, we were one. She surrounded me, and I surrounded her, and the rest of the world fell away. My entire life, every moment, every choice was leading to this, this night where I loved her and she loved me.

Anna's hand found mine, lacing our fingers together as we moved. My free hand tangled in sunset curls, balancing on my elbow.

There was a wave coming. The crest that was building far too quickly. I wasn't ready for the break, not just yet. Fighting to hold it back was futile. I was going to drown in Anna. That fact was all right, delightful even, just as long as I took her with me—and I did—we were swept away together, lost to ecstasy and everything I'd ever wanted.

Reality came back slowly. Somehow, I'd ended up on my back with Anna splayed atop me in a pile of limbs and fiery hair. I dragged fingertips through her curls, smoothing the tangles I'd created while we fought for breath.

"So..." she breathed. "The maids undersold it quite a bit."

A huffed chuckle escaped me, and she rose and fell with my chest. "That was... incredible."

"We were, weren't we?" she asked, propping her chin on my chest.

"No surprise there. We've always been perfect together."

In response, Anna dropped a kiss to my chest before settling back down in the crook of my arm with a thoughtful hum.

"Quite the day, both of our dreams came true. Bakery for you, you for me..." I said as I pressed a kiss to the sunset curls on the crown of her head.

"Augie... *You've* always been my dream. The bakery is just a bonus."

Speech was beyond me. I swallowed back the knot in my throat and the unshed tears with a wordless acknowledgment. And I fell asleep, the girl with hair like sunset who smelled of pastry and home wrapped safely in my arms. And it was better than I'd ever imagined.

Epilogue

THE SUNRISE FIT in my hands.

I had only felt this awe once before in my life, the first time I saw the girl with the sunset curls tied back in a dusky purple ribbon.

My little sunrise was pressed against my chest, nuzzling closer, seeking warmth. With bright gold wisps of hair and a hint of burnt-orange undertones, she was her mother's daughter. The gray-green of her eyes matched her mother's as well. Her little hand was wrapped around my thumb, five tiny, perfect fingers. Her fist might as well have been wrapped around my heart. It was the only explanation for how thoroughly she had me under her spell.

We rocked slowly in the chair by the window long after I finished my story. My words drifted away some time ago when my daughter fell into a restful sleep. Those memories were best enjoyed in silence, lest I wake my sweet audience.

The sunrise, the one for poor men who weren't me, was brushing across the sky. Anna was still soundly asleep across the room, exhausted from her efforts yesterday. Tired from bringing me my little sunrise, my Emma.

She smacked her lips sleepily, fussing just the littlest bit. I suspected she would want her mother soon, but I shushed her quietly, hoping she would allow a few more minutes of sleep. "Mama is resting, little sunrise."

"Mama is awake." Anna's tired voice washed over us from the bed. I glanced up to see her perfect green eyes filled with love. Reluctantly, I stood and handed over my precious bundle. "Papa is a terrible storyteller, little one. Almost none of that was true."

My gasp may have been feigned. "It was the absolute truth."

"Perhaps as much as thirty percent of it was true. At least you didn't tell her anything too inappropriate."

"No, I lulled her to sleep long before I reached that point."

"Well, a few decades will do that to a girl. The waiting certainly put me to sleep. Did you set her down even once?" She asked.

"I don't want her to be lonely." Anna just smiled indulgently at me.

"How do you propose to return to the club in two months' time?"

"I can stop reprobates from cheating while cuddling."

"Well, that's good because I certainly cannot bake while cuddling." She shifted Emma to a breast with ease.

"We have it all sorted. Your mom will care for her for the few hours our work hours overlap. I don't want you fretting while you're trying to heal."

"I suspect fretting is part of being a parent. Mama did well with us, though, didn't she?"

"Seems like it, and I'm sure this little one will be much less troublesome than we were."

"I suspect you're delusional, but I applaud your optimism. She already has you convinced of her perfection. You will let her get away with all sorts of mischief."

"Look at her. She is perfection."

Anna peered down at our daughter with awe.

"We did all right, didn't we?"

"You did more than all right. I did almost none of the work."

"True. Augie?" I brushed my daughter's golden, copper curls with one hand.

"Yes?"

"You were right. All of my best days have been with you."

"Yesterday might have been the very best. It's all downhill from here."

"I doubt that," she whispered, stroking Emma's hair. "Didn't you say you wanted more than one of these?"

"Oh, that was before I saw what you went through yesterday. I won't make it through that a second time. Besides, we've created perfection on our first attempt." Said tiny bundle of perfection had curled back to sleep on Anna's chest with a few tired lip smacks.

"If you say so."

I pressed a gentle kiss to her temple. Anna quickly fell asleep with Emma in her arms. Sunrise and sunset curled together as one.

The End

The Most Imprudent Matches series will continue with Hugh and Kate's story:
Winning my Wife

To see your favorite moments from Anna's perspective, you can find bonus scenes allyhudson.com/bonus-scenes

Acknowledgments

Thank you to *all* my friends and family for your support in this and all my projects.

Thank you to my mother, for your willingness to talk through all my plot holes.

Thank you to Martha for reminding me to see the sun on occasion.

Thank you, as always, to Bryton for putting up with me and my complaints on a regular basis.

Thank you to Mariah for pretending my first drafts are good.

Thank you to Rebecca Sanchez at Once Upon an Editor for whipping this into shape.

Thank you Holly Perret at The Swoonies Romance Art for my breathtaking cover.

And thank you to everyone who has ever had to taste test my baking experiments.

About the Author

Ally Hudson was raised in Hudson, Ohio. Currently, she resides in Fort Wayne, Indiana, with a very sassy dog. *The Baker and the Bookmaker* is the second book in her Most Imprudent Matches series. She writes of cinnamon-bun heroes, snarky friendships, and true love. Her other hobbies include reading, embroidery, and re-watching television shows she has seen ten times already.

Printed in Great Britain
by Amazon